TRAINING TOMMY

TRAINING TOMMY

•

Barbara Meyers

AVALON BOOKS
NEW YORK

Mey

PRINTED IN THE UNITED STATES OF AMERICA
ON ACID-FREE PAPER
BY HADDON CRAFTSMEN, BLOOMSBURG, PENNSYLVANIA

For Mom and Dad, with love

Special thanks to
Sandra Lee Carmouche
Jennifer Grant
Jean Harrington

Chapter One

"Come in," Sabrina called at the sound of the doorbell. The soothing music on the yoga videotape did not disguise the sound of Elaine's footsteps on the polished hardwood floor.

"You're late, ohmmmmm," she informed her friend from her undignified position, lying on her back with her ankles next to her ears, toes touching the mat above her head.

"Sorry, I didn't know you were expecting me," came an amused and unfamiliar male voice.

Sabrina gasped and rolled to a standing position so quickly she miscalculated her momentum and she toppled against the stranger. He backpedaled to avoid a head-on collision and tripped over the Persian cat, Victoria, falling to the floor and taking Sabrina with him.

Victoria fled to the relative safety of a nearby rocking chair for a moment to determine what the fuss was about,

1

then leapt back down to sniff the stranger's ankles as if that would explain his presence.

Just as Sabrina was about to rise, a monstrous multicolored dog barreled through the open front door and headed straight for Victoria. The cat yowled in outrage and darted into the dining room, the dog hot on her tail.

So much for relaxation, Sabrina thought.

Still slightly disoriented, she didn't know who or what to deal with first. The man stirred beneath her. She slid away from him and carefully got to her feet. He wasn't faring much better than she was. He groaned as he grasped the side of the coffee table and used it to push himself to a sitting position.

Victoria whizzed by, headed for the stairs, the dog barking joyously as he bounded after her.

"Oh, my goodness."

Sabrina glanced at the man. He was rubbing the back of his neck and rolling his shoulders, making sure everything was still in working order.

She started for the stairs, but hesitated. How could she leave a stranger, possibly injured, in her living room? She halted and turned back to him.

He waved her in the direction of the stairs as if he'd read her mind. "Go on. I'll be all right."

"Are you sure?"

"Positive."

Just as she touched the bottom step, the duet raced by at full speed. She pressed herself against the wall as visions of the dog flattening her with his size and weight danced before her eyes.

She followed them as they disappeared into the dining room once again. The unmistakable clatter of china against glass warned her of their location. She reached out to steady the china hutch as Victoria huddled beneath it.

"That's enough!" she addressed the dog. "Cease and desist this instant, or—or, I'll call the dogcatcher on you." *Was there a worse threat for a canine,* Sabrina wondered. *And if so, what might it be?*

She heard Victoria hiss and for once was sorry the cat had been declawed. She'd never thought poor Victoria would have to defend herself in her own home.

The dog lowered his chest to the floor, leaving his rear end up in the air, bushy tail wagging in excitement. She could hear him panting as he pushed his nose even further beneath the hutch. She saw Victoria's tail twitching in outrage at the edge of the cabinet as the cat growled in warning.

"Okay. That's enough." She hooked her fingers under the dog's collar and tugged. His nose was buried beneath the edge of the cabinet and he didn't move an inch. "Now listen, you, I don't know where you came from, but wherever it is, you're going back." She tugged harder. "Just as soon as I can get you pointed in the other direction."

Sheer force had no impact on the animal. She changed tactics. Releasing his collar, she stroked his more than ample fur. "Nice doggie. There's a good boy. You don't want to scare the little kitty, do you? Huh? Come on, boy." Sabrina suddenly realized she was making an assumption as to the dog's gender without all the facts admitted into evidence, but she wasn't about to investigate further at the moment.

"How about a nice doggie treat, huh?" she crooned. "What do you say? A biscuit? A bone? I've got some turkey breast in the refrigerator. I'll give you a slice if you leave my cat alone."

Perhaps she should offer him the entire breast of turkey instead of just one slice? She tried the tug on the collar again. "Come on. Out of there," she commanded as she pulled. "You are really . . . starting to . . . annoy me." She put all her effort into pulling the dog away from the cabinet.

"Skid, come here."

The dog sprang back so suddenly at the command from the stranger she'd left in the living room that he knocked Sabrina onto her backside. On her way down she bumped her head on the solid oak dining table, but she hardly noticed as she watched the dog trot over to the stranger and gaze up at him adoringly.

Sprawled on the floor, Sabrina stared at them. "He's yours?"

The two of them looked at her with expressions of interest. She noticed they both had brown eyes. The man nodded and Sabrina was sure she saw amusement flicker across his features. He extended a hand and helped her up.

"I'm Tommy Cameron. I just moved in next door. And this is Skid." He scratched the dog behind his ears. The dog moaned in ecstasy. "You must be Sabrina Talbott. Are you okay?"

"How did you . . . why are you . . . what do you . . . ?"

Tommy held up a hand and finished her incomplete questions, counting them off on his fingers. "How did I know your name? Your former neighbors, the McDermotts, mentioned it. Why am I here? I came by to ask if I could possibly borrow an extension cord. I'm having a party tonight and I don't quite have all my stereo equipment hooked up." It took him a little longer to figure out the last one. He narrowed his eyes in concentration. Skid cocked his head, gazing up at her. "What do you . . . think you're doing?"

Sabrina returned her gaze from the dog to her new neighbor, forgetting that he was completing *her* sentences.

"Looking at your dog."

"I thought that's what you were going to ask me."

"You know there's an uncanny resemblance between the two of you."

Tommy brushed a handful of wavy brown hair back from his forehead. "I know we both need haircuts, but no one's yet told me I look like my dog."

"Oh, no, I didn't mean . . . that exactly." Sabrina gulped in a deep breath as she took a really good look at Tommy Cameron. A faded blue T-shirt stretched across his broad chest and hugged his biceps. Equally well-worn jeans covered the rest of him, including his muscular-looking thighs. A pair of beat-up, no-longer-white sneakers completed his ensemble.

"I meant, uh, mannerisms, the expression on his face."

Tommy glanced down at Skid, and Skid turned his head in Tommy's direction. Tommy shook his head. Skid did the same. "Sorry. I still don't see the resemblance."

Sabrina gave up. "Never mind. An extension cord, you said? I think I have one in the kitchen."

He followed her there. "Nice house," he commented.

"Thank you. It was my grandmother's before she died."

She took an extension cord from a drawer and handed it to him.

"Nice outfit." His appreciative gaze swept over her form-fitting leotard and tights. Sabrina knew she was covered more than if she were wearing a swimsuit, but somehow she felt exposed in the face of Tommy's interest.

Virile male has breached the neutral zone, her internal alarm system shouted.

"Thank you." She felt her skin start to prickle the way

it always did when she was nervous. Tommy Cameron made her nervous. She didn't like it. Not one bit.

"Was there anything else?"

"No," he replied after a beat. "Not at the moment."

She followed him to the front door. Skid trotted out, fluffy tail waving like a flag made of troll's hair.

Tommy paused at the bottom of the porch steps and turned back, one foot on the last step. "So anyway, I'm having sort of a housewarming party later. Why don't you stop over?"

Sabrina shook her head. "I don't usually attend parties unless I'm helping with the catering. Besides, I, um, have other plans."

"You're a caterer? I thought Mr. McDermott said you're a—"

"Teacher. I am. High school English. And I'm definitely not a caterer, but I have a friend who is. She calls me whenever she's shorthanded, usually around the Christmas holidays. Mostly what I do is help the hostess."

"Or host?" Tommy asked, his eyes alive with interest.

Sabrina's skin prickled again. "Or host, I suppose. Although around here, it's usually wives who plan the parties."

Tommy grinned. "Well, I don't have a wife . . . yet. But I will pretty soon."

"Oh? Really? How—nice." *What* was this nagging sense of disappointment she felt at *that* announcement? She'd just met Tommy Cameron. Why should she care if he was in the middle of planning his wedding? She could tell just by his appearance, he certainly wasn't *her* type.

Oh, no. She knew exactly the kind of man she wanted. Mr. Perfect would be secure and stable. He'd be a professional, a banker or a lawyer maybe, and he'd wear a tailored suit to work every day. He'd get a haircut every six weeks. If he had a dog, it would be a civilized creature, well groomed and well trained. A Lhasa apso perhaps. Or a Maltese. Yes. She kind of liked those little dogs, with their silky hair and pleasant dispositions.

She frowned as she glanced over Tommy Cameron's shoulder to see the beast named Skid showing a bit too much interest in the base of one of her favorite rosebushes. Why would anyone name a dog Skid? "Uh, Mr. Cameron—"

"Oh, come *on*." Tommy groaned. "Not Mr. Cameron. Tommy. Just Tommy, okay?"

"Okay, *Tommy*. Do you have a leash for your dog?"

"Well, yeah, somewhere. I may not have unpacked it."

She took a couple of steps forward as the dog pawed the ground. "Don't you dare," she warned him.

"Unpack his leash?"

"Not you," Sabrina replied. "Him." She pointed to Skid. "That was my grandmother's prizewinning rose garden. You'll have to contain your dog. There's a leash law in Ruskin County, you know."

"Sure. No problem. Skid, come here." The dog glanced at Tommy, then went back to inspecting the rosebush.

"Skid. Come here, buddy. Come on," Tommy encouraged. He patted his thigh. Skid ignored him.

Tommy walked over, hooked two fingers under Skid's collar, and bent toward him. "You're making me look bad in front of the lady," he hissed.

Sabrina hid her smile, not knowing if he'd meant for her to overhear or not.

He straightened as he returned to the front walk.

"If he digs any of them up—" she began.

"He won't," Tommy assured her.

"But if he does . . ."

"I'll replace them, I promise."

Sabrina nodded. "Okay. Enjoy your party."

"I wish you'd come. Skid and I promise to be on our best behavior."

Sabrina had a feeling that Tommy Cameron's idea of "best behavior" and hers were probably two very different things. "Thanks, but I doubt I'll be able to make it."

She went back inside and closed the door. Her last glimpse of her neighbor was his smile of farewell tinged with disappointment. She could swear the dog was smiling too, only in Skid's case, his tongue lolled out of his mouth and he appeared unfazed by her rejection.

Chapter Two

Tommy loped back to his house, dog in tow. So much for making a good first impression. "No thanks to you," he told Skid as they gained the front porch. Skid wagged his tail and looked up at Tommy with adoration in his eyes.

Tommy opened the door and Skid trotted in, not a care in the world. In the kitchen, Tommy took a dog biscuit from a box on the counter and held it up.

"Sit," he commanded. Skid circled around in a happy dance then barked sharply.

"Stand still."

Skid jumped up and made a grab for the biscuit. Tommy held it out of his reach. Skid moaned pitifully.

"Roll over, you big galoot!"

Skid gave a sharp insistent bark, put his paws on Tommy's chest, and licked his chin. Tommy grinned and scratched him behind the ears. He lowered the biscuit and

Skid snatched it from his fingers. "You know what your problem is?" he asked the dog. "You don't listen."

Satisfied with his treat, Skid dropped back down to all fours, relocated to a patch of linoleum warmed by the sun shining through the window, and plopped down.

Tommy started to unpack the half-empty boxes of kitchen items. "You can't just go barging into a lady's house," he informed Skid. Skid gave him a skeptical look as if to say, "Isn't that what you did?"

"And you can't go chasing her cat around either."

Skid thumped his tail a couple of times.

Tommy frowned. "And another thing." He bent toward the dog and shook a finger at him. "Don't get any ideas about digging up that rosebush you were so interested in. When I call, you come. Got it?"

Skid sighed and blinked his eyes a couple of times before closing them completely.

Tommy set the empty box near the back door and started on the next one. "Ah ha!" He held up Skid's leash. "I'm sure our new neighbor will be happy to know I've found this." Skid opened one eye, then promptly closed it.

Tommy hung the leash on a hook near the door, thoughts of impressing his neighbor with his well-behaved dog running through his head. He glanced over at Skid. Well-behaved might be too much to hope for. Restrained he could probably manage.

Sabrina Talbott would certainly consider it an improvement.

The McDermotts hadn't mentioned how attractive Sabrina was. Even now, Tommy could picture her sparkly eyes—a mix of lavender and blue that reminded him of tanzanite. Her dark hair, which looked like it had that silky sort of texture that just fell through your fingers, had been slightly mussed from her yoga session. The leotard left no doubt Sabrina Talbott took very good care of herself.

If only she had agreed to come to his party tonight. He could make a much better impression.

That night Sabrina lay in bed for over an hour while music from Tommy Cameron's stereo system reverberated through the neighborhood. All of the old homes along Broadleaf Lane had been built in a style popular in the Midwest in the 1940s: two stories of brick or painted clapboard, with deep front porches and smaller stoops in back, on small lots. Tommy's house was so close to hers, in fact, not even thirty feet separated them.

Closing her bedroom windows succeeded in blocking out the evening breeze of the late summer night but did nothing to squelch the pounding rock tunes delivered by speakers worthy of a head-banger rock band. The sounds coming from next door pounded in rhythm with the slight throb in her head from when she'd hit it on the table earlier.

For Pete's sake! She had three tutoring sessions scheduled for tomorrow morning and an SAT preparation class in the afternoon. How was she ever going to get to sleep?

By marching over to Tommy Cameron's house and requesting that he turn the music down, that's how. She flipped the covers back and rolled out of bed. Yanking off her nightgown, she grabbed the shorts and T-shirt she'd worn earlier in the day. If all went well she'd be back in her nightgown—back in her *quiet* bedroom—in a few short minutes. Just as soon as she explained proper neighborhood etiquette to Tommy Cameron.

She couldn't be the only neighbor being kept awake by the noise, could she? What about the Arnolds on the other side? And the Wilsons across the street? Surely they were just as disturbed by the loud music.

She hesitated at the edge of her property. The night air was relatively warm for the end of August in rural Illinois. A slight breeze blew a strand of hair across her eyes and she brushed it away as she surveyed the scene before her.

Several of Tommy's guests were crowded around his front porch and steps, holding plastic cups, chatting and laughing. They all appeared relaxed, enjoying each other's company. She fought down the nervousness she always felt in crowds of unfamiliar people.

As a guest, she never fit in at parties. Inevitably, she would leave them feeling she'd worn the wrong outfit or said the wrong thing to the wrong person. Growing up with a mother and stepfather who were champion party people, she thought she would have grown used to the forced gaiety and loud voices. But she never had. She preferred her role as occasional assistant to the hostess so she could melt into the background and not feel obligated to mingle.

Steeling herself, she stepped forward. The group gathered on the porch barely paid any attention as she squeezed by them. And why would they? In a T-shirt and shorts, for once she blended right in with the rest of the crowd.

She knocked on the screen door, and a fellow standing just inside opened it for her. He did it automatically, never breaking eye contact with his female companion.

Really! Sabrina thought. Anyone could just walk into this party, invited or not. It made her think of the party scenes in those teen movies. People just showed up and were allowed in whether they belonged there or not. Evidently, Tommy Cameron was no more discriminating in his choice of guests than those teens.

Where was he? She gazed at the sea of unfamiliar faces

as she wound her way from room to room. Tommy Cameron might not be an attentive host, but his guests were having a good time.

Several board games were in progress. The dining room had been turned into a billiards hall. A dartboard hung at the end of the hallway, evidently the perfect distance for a competitive match.

Everywhere there were clusters of people. Empty pizza boxes were scattered here and there along with potato chip bags and fried chicken buckets.

The atmosphere reminded her of the one and only frat party she'd attended at college. Competitive games of pool and darts. Loud music and throngs of guests gesturing and laughing.

The Arnolds and the Wilsons weren't complaining about the loud music because she spotted them in a cluster together near the back door.

Emily Wilson waggled her fingers at Sabrina. "Hi, Sabrina. I was wondering if I'd see you here. I know you usually avoid parties like the plague," she teased in a half-yell.

She knew Emily was joking with her, but as usual, Sabrina couldn't think of an appropriate response.

"Hey, Sabrina, great party, huh?" Lori Arnold chimed in. Her husband Drew leaned forward to greet her, as did Emily's husband, Ron.

Then they all fell silent. Sabrina felt as though a spotlight were shining on her. As the newcomer, it was her turn to speak. "You wouldn't happen to know where I could find, uh, Tommy, would you?" she asked them. She felt slightly uncomfortable referring to her new neighbor so informally. Tommy seemed almost like, well, a pet name. One she would normally reserve for someone she knew extremely well. Or for a very young child.

"Ah ha!" Emily responded. "I knew he'd catch your eye. You are one lucky girl, Sabrina. You don't even have to go looking for Mr. Perfect. He moved in right next door to you."

Sabrina winced. Tommy Cameron? Mr. Perfect? Boy, was Emily off base on that one.

"I need to ask him something. Have you seen him?" Sabrina absently rubbed at the small bump on the side of her head.

"Last I saw him, he was in the den back there," Drew said in a near shout. He jerked his head to indicate the general vicinity of the den.

"Thanks, Drew."

Sabrina squeezed through the clusters of people and finally located Tommy at the back of the house. Computer equipment covered nearly every corner of the room, some of it obviously in the process of being set up. He and a couple of other men were gathered around a partially constructed shelving unit.

Sabrina approached and Tommy's head came up as if he had radar detection. His eyes lit up with interest. Or was that her imagination? Maybe she'd been reading too many romance novels. He gave her a boyish grin of delight, dropped the instruction sheet, and stepped toward her.

"You came after all. I was hoping you would." His gaze swept up and down her casual attire. "You look great." He sniffed. "You smell good too. Want a drink?"

All of this he said loud enough to make himself heard over the music. He took her hand and led her toward the kitchen. Sabrina followed his lead. Maybe the kitchen would be slightly quieter. She could explain her mission there.

She didn't plan on staying. She didn't need anything to drink.

He had a plastic cup in his hand. "How about something soft? Club soda? Ginger ale?" He snapped his fingers. "I bet you're a root beer kind of girl."

He half-filled the cup with ice, twisted the top off a bottle of root beer, and poured.

Sabrina didn't know what else to do but accept it when he handed it to her. "I wanted to talk to you," she said loudly.

Tommy held a hand to his ear. "What?"

"I said I wanted to talk to you about the—"

He shook his head and walked away.

How rude!

Drink in hand, Sabrina trotted after him.

"Frankie! Frankie!" he yelled, giving one of his guests a friendly shove in the direction of the stereo. "Turn that music off, would you! I've had about all of Metallica I can stand. Put on something we can dance to."

Frankie turned off the loud music. The guests quieted in anticipation, all eyes on Frankie as he selected a CD and loaded it. Slow dance music poured forth. Somebody dimmed the lights. Couples found each other.

Tommy set Sabrina's drink aside and took her hand. "Dance with me. Now that you're here."

Her mouth went dry and a protest rose to her lips. Dancing with Tommy Cameron hadn't been her intention at all. She'd wanted him to turn the music down. Period. Well, he'd done that. Mission accomplished.

She gazed around at the other couples clinging together. Tommy tugged on her hand, catching her off guard all over again with that smile and those eyes. "Come on. I don't bite."

He held her hand in his, and his other arm came around her back. Sabrina followed his lead, her objections on hold for the moment. What were those objections anyway?

Tommy's presence surrounded her, enveloped her. Her brain stopped functioning and her senses came alive. The warmth of his hand splayed across her back sent waves of heat through her. She caught his scent—an odd but not unpleasant mix of dog, from his roughhousing with Skid, she supposed, and laundry detergent, or maybe fabric softener, from his clothes—underlying both was the unmistakable scent of man.

Sabrina's fingers clenched where they curved around his shoulder. In response he pulled her closer, his head bent over hers. Her hand felt lost in his bigger one. He caressed the nape of her neck and then further down her spine.

Her breath caught in her throat. Tommy Cameron interested her. How dare he! The nerve of the man! With his overgrown dog and his loud parties, his too-long hair and his well-worn T-shirts and jeans.

The song ended and Sabrina pulled back. She meant to look at Tommy's face but her attention focused itself on his broad chest instead. Finally she moved her chin up and met his eyes. He'd released her hand and encircled her with both arms. His smile nearly made her faint where she stood.

Another slow song started. She couldn't be attracted to Tommy Cameron. She wouldn't allow it. She'd accomplished her mission, she reminded herself. The music was no longer so loud she wouldn't be able to sleep. So what if thoughts of her new neighbor kept her awake instead? He'd never know.

Chapter Three

"**I**—have to go." She didn't even stop to think what Emily Post might say about such an abrupt exit.

Tommy nodded. "Bathroom's right through there. Next to the kitchen."

"What?" How come his hands were still holding hers? Why hadn't she left yet? Why couldn't she pull her gaze away from his?

"The bathroom?" Tommy prompted.

"Oh. No." Sabrina had a master's degree in English, but she suddenly couldn't seem to remember any words in that language that had more than one syllable.

"No? Great." Tommy wrapped his arms around her and started moving again. "Boy, you smell good." That was probably due to the lavender bath salts she'd soaked in before attempting to get some sleep earlier.

"So do you." Her nose was almost flattened against the

front of his T-shirt. She allowed herself a wonderful, brief fantasy of dancing with Tommy Cameron for the rest of the night.

"I'm really glad you came."

She had to remember that Tommy Cameron was not Mr. Perfect. He struck her as a tad immature. Maybe a bit irresponsible. Tommy reminded her of her stepfather, Ted. A fun-loving military officer who'd moved her and her mother from one location to another as his assignments changed. A man whose brilliant career in the service barely eclipsed his reputation for being the life of the party.

She could hear the same reprimands she'd heard all her life echo through her mind: Lighten up, Sabrina. Have a little fun, Sabrina. But what did her mother and her new husband know? After their marriage, they yanked six-year-old Sabrina out of school and dragged her around the globe with them. She'd hated every minute of it: Leaving her beloved kitten behind, the only pet she'd ever had as a child. The impermanence of base housing, the new schools. Her parents' nonstop entertaining no matter where they were.

Her mother and stepfather constantly cajoled her to lighten up and have fun, until finally one day in frustration she screamed at both of them, "This is not fun for me. I will never have fun!"

From that moment forward she'd had one goal—stability. She obtained her education and chose a solid career as a teacher. She purposely surrounded herself with serious people who stayed in one place. Thanks to her grandmother, she inherited a home of her own in a quiet neighborhood. Here she kept reminders of her earliest childhood. Even her grandmother's snooty cat, Victoria, took the place of that long-ago kitten she'd had to leave behind. She was more than content with the stability she'd created for herself while she waited for Mr. Perfect to come along.

Until Tommy Cameron kissed her.

She'd been lost in her thoughts, relaxed in his arms, automatically swaying to the music. When had he changed the tune? How had his hands repositioned themselves to cup her face? How had he managed to tilt her face up to his without her realizing it? His lips touched hers, and she took a quick startled breath.

He hesitated for a fraction of a second. He gave her a chance to put a halt to his advances, but she didn't take it. What was wrong with her? He kissed her again. They were in the middle of the living room, surrounded by other couples. The music was still going strong, but she and Tommy were no longer dancing.

She was drowning. Drowning in that kiss. His lips were warm and tasted faintly of ginger ale. Sabrina almost forgot to breathe.

Red alert! Red alert! her subconscious warned. Involvement imminent! Involvement imminent! Retreat! Retreat!

Breathless, Sabrina somehow managed to end the kiss. She stared up at Tommy. His eyes blazed down at her.

She disentangled herself from him. "I have to go," she whispered.

This time she took a couple of steps back, turned, and fled.

She flew across the lawn as if Skid and ten of his canine buddies were chasing her. She flung open the door of her house, startling Victoria who yelped in outrage.

Sabrina locked the door and pounded up the stairs where she changed back into her nightgown in the dark and jumped back in bed. She pulled the covers up to her chin and lay there, her heart beating a mile a minute as if she'd just awakened from a nightmare and didn't know what to make of it.

I can't be attracted to that man, she told herself. *I simply can't.* Just look at him! The unruly dog. The houseful of people. The pool table and the dartboard. She'd also noticed a big-screen TV. She could just imagine the crowd that would gather at Tommy's house during football season. And basketball season. And hockey season. He probably even had a satellite system.

Then there was Tommy's state-of-the-art stereo. With its multitude of buttons and blinking lights, surely it belonged at NASA headquarters. She blamed it for her current predicament.

She rolled over and buried her face in her pillow. *Stop it! Stop it! Stop it!* she warned herself. Stop thinking about Tommy Cameron. And his kiss. Especially his kiss.

When Sabrina arrived home the following afternoon a potted rosebush sat on her front walk. As she approached to investigate, Tommy appeared around the corner of her house, shovel in hand.

She glanced from the rosebush to Tommy and back. It appeared to be a healthy specimen.

He leaned on the handle of his shovel. "I was hoping to plant that before you got back."

Speaking of healthy specimens. Sabrina drank in the sight of him. He probably had a closetful of T-shirts, faded blue jeans, and sneakers. And if they all fit him they way these did, he probably had a closetful of women drooling over him as well. Speaking of drooling. . . .

Sabrina licked her lips in an automatic reaction. She had to stop this. She had to stop reacting to Tommy like she was sixteen with her first romantic crush. Someone had to be the adult here. "We've just met and already you're buying me roses?" Oh, no. Was she flirting with him? *What* was wrong with her?

Tommy chuckled. "Uh, well, Skid sort of got away from me this morning, and, well." He stepped back and pointed to a disturbed patch of earth. The prizewinner that Skid had shown such interest in yesterday was nowhere in sight.

Sabrina raised an eyebrow. No. She wouldn't say it. No matter how much she wanted to. She absolutely would not say it. Yes she would. "I told you so."

Tommy ducked his head in acknowledgment.

"You're right. It's my fault. I was on the phone, and I don't have a latch for the front screen yet. Skid tends to dart out at inopportune times."

"Hmmmm. Yes. I see." Brilliant, Sabrina. Impress him with your extensive vocabulary. "Perhaps you'd like to discuss this over tea?"

"Tea?"

Oh no, had she really invited her new neighbor to tea? Something was seriously wrong with her thought processes. Ten feet within Tommy Cameron's range and her brain refused to function.

She shrugged. "It's something I do sometimes in the afternoons."

"You drink tea. In the afternoon."

Her "teas"-for-one were a well-kept secret. She blushed. "That's okay. Never mind. You wouldn't understand." Her grandmother, Mamie Talbott, had introduced her to the concept of afternoon tea. Whenever Sabrina visited, her grandmother always made it special with tiny sandwiches and buttery cookies or crumpets. She now found the tea ritual soothing after a challenging day spent in the company of teenagers.

She walked up the porch steps and unlocked the door. Tommy followed her. "What's to understand? So what if you like to drink tea in the afternoon? My old man liked to stop off for something a little stronger every afternoon."

She'd issued the invitation without thinking and tried to retract it so Tommy wouldn't feel compelled to join her. But when she opened the door, he was right behind her. He seemed to fill up the entryway with his presence.

If he laughed at her tea ritual, she swore it would be the last time he'd ever cross her threshold.

She set her things down and he trailed behind her to the kitchen. She could sense him glancing around, getting more of a feel for her home than he had yesterday.

Once she set the kettle on to boil, she set out the tea tray and slid two crumpets into the toaster oven. In the dining room she selected a teapot from her grandmother's precious collection.

She was aware the entire time of Tommy's gaze following her every move. Victoria made an appearance and approached Tommy warily, delicately sniffing his shoes and ankles. "Cool cat," he commented. He hunkered down to pet her. Normally skittish around strangers, Victoria made no objection as Tommy stroked her fur, nor did she complain when he scooped her up in his arms and straightened, rubbing her absentmindedly under the chin.

"Did you get lost on your way back from the bathroom last night?" he asked after she poured water into the pot and covered it with one of Grandmother Mamie's cozies.

Tommy had won over the normally aloof Victoria in record time. Sabrina glared at the traitorous cat while Victoria purred in contentment and ignored her.

Sabrina looked directly at Tommy. He needed a haircut.

Or at least an introduction to a hairbrush. His warm brown eyes gazed at her and she forgot the question.

"What?"

"You said you had to go. And then you never came back."

"I needed to go home."

"Why?"

Sabrina turned to fuss with the tray, rearranging the spoons and adjusting the cups in their saucers. *Why* had she invited Tommy to tea? "Because," she said at last.

"Because why?"

Sabrina moved the crumpets from the toaster to the tray. Tommy set Victoria down and followed her to the tea table in the living room. She poured the tea and set a cup and crumpet in front of him.

All the while possible answers flitted through her mind. *Because I don't like parties. Because the only reason I was there in the first place was to get you to turn the music down. Because I've been thinking about your kiss all day.*

She felt a blush creep up her throat to her cheeks and hoped Tommy wouldn't notice.

"You left just when things were mellowing out." Tommy dumped two spoonfuls of sugar into his tea and stirred. He picked up the cup, and Sabrina found herself fascinated by the way his big hands cradled the delicate china.

"I told you I'm not much of a party person." Her eyes met his as he returned the cup to the saucer.

"What's this?" He peered down at the crumpet as if it were a foreign object.

"It's a crumpet."

"Really? Is that what Little Miss Muffett ate? No, wait,

that was curds and whey. 'Little Miss Muffett sat on her crumpet, eating her curds and whey.' "

Sabrina felt a smile curving her lips. "That was a tuffet, I believe."

"A tuffet? Got any of those around?"

Sabrina giggled. Maybe she really was just sixteen again.

"Okay, then, let me try the crumpet." He slathered butter and marmalade on it and took a bite.

Sabrina sipped her tea and watched him. He washed the last bit down with the rest of his tea.

His gaze swept the tray as if searching for further sustenance. Finding none he looked at her. "So why aren't you a party person? You don't like to have fun?"

Sabrina was back in control of herself. The comfort of her tea ritual had helped. "Let's just say your idea of fun and my idea of fun are probably not the same thing."

"I can think of at least one thing we both enjoy."

"A true gentlemen wouldn't even mention it. Since you did, let me say for the record, that kiss didn't mean a thing. It—it was the root beer."

"You didn't drink any root beer. And just for the record, I was going to say we both enjoy *dancing*."

Nonplussed, Sabrina sat back in her chair and glowered at the man across the table.

"Thanks for the tea and the tuffet. Uh, crumpet." He scooted his chair back. "I'll go plant your rosebush now."

"It's kind of late in the season to be planting a rosebush."

Tommy stood up. "I'm sorry about that, but I told you I'd replace anything Skid dug up."

Sabrina followed him. "I'm sorry. I shouldn't have implied that you weren't a gentlemen."

Tommy stopped just on the other side of the door. "Don't

apologize. But give me some credit. I recognize a lady when I meet one."

He stepped off the porch and Sabrina closed the door, struck by an unaccustomed sense of emptiness.

Chapter Four

Sunday afternoon Sabrina donned her gardening clothes. The roses were in desperate need of some attention before they went to sleep for the winter.

She breathed the warm air deeply as she gathered her tools. Soon the leaves would start to turn and fall. She and her neighbors would rake them into piles, which the children would scatter with their play. Fireplaces would be put into use. There'd be hayrides and bonfires and football games. A sense of excitement tickled her at the start of every school year, for it signaled the fall season. She loved the rituals she could count on throughout the year, which was why she loved teaching. She taught the same classes, yet to the students a new world opened up for them. The beauty of English literature: poetry, plays, essays, novels.

In her overalls and clogs, she crossed the porch to the front walk and surveyed the bushes. Several were still in bloom, though their colors were fading. All of them needed pruning or deadheading.

A clatter next door snagged her attention. Tommy and several other men, a few she recognized from the party, had gathered in the front yard. One of them tossed a football up in the air and caught it.

She watched the guys shove each other a bit and then separate into two teams. Scenes from the movie *Animal House* ran through her mind, making her shiver.

She hadn't realized until now how much she missed the McDermotts. Almost as soon as Sabrina moved in, they'd adopted her as their surrogate child. Before hip-replacement surgery slowed him down, retired Mr. McDermott always seemed to be looking for handyman projects to keep himself busy. He'd hung a trellis along her back porch last spring. The year before he'd replaced the worn locks on her windows. Mrs. McDermott regularly tempted Sabrina with offerings of home-baked goodies.

Still, no matter how often her neighbors changed, she would never leave this place. Her haven was a legacy from her Grandmother Mamie Talbott, along with the antiques that filled it, her beloved rose garden, and her snooty Persian cat.

The house wasn't as big as some of the others on the street, but it was hers now. She felt connected to her grandmother as she worked hard to maintain Mamie's standards for home and hearth. The windowpanes sparkled in the late August sunshine. The polished oak door gleamed. The clipped green grass stood at attention. Not one dandelion reared its ugly yellow head.

She caressed the petals of a soft pink tea rose, annoyed at the loss of the bush Skid had dug up. Even though she wasn't as skilled a gardener as her grandmother, she hoped it wasn't too late for her hydrangeas and lilies to flower as well, along with the peonies and four o'clocks. Mamie had worked hard to have a flower garden like those of her British forebears. Sabrina wanted nothing more than to carry on the tradition. Her new neighbor and his dog weren't making it any easier.

A shout went up from the group on the lawn next door. The men pushed and shoved each other. A couple of them landed on the ground. Tommy came barreling across *her* lawn. Her mouth dropped open in surprise. He stopped abruptly, his gaze on her.

"Look out!" someone shouted.

She turned in time to see a football spiraling toward her.

When it hit, Sabrina saw stars, instinctively covered her eye with her hand, and wobbled unsteadily for a moment. Tommy caught her before she hit the ground.

"Oh, wow. Sorry about that. Are you okay?" He peered down at her and Sabrina stared back at him with one eye.

He glanced up as the others loped across her lawn. "Nice pass, Joey," he said.

Joey grinned. "Yeah, it was." He nodded in Sabrina's direction. "Are we calling pass interference on her?"

A couple of the other guys chuckled and Tommy scowled as he hunkered down next to her. "Let me see." He moved her hand away from her eye and winced. "Ouch."

Sabrina wondered if she was in shock. On some level she was aware of a throbbing pain in the vicinity of her left eye and cheekbone. But she was much more aware of Tommy's mesmerizing brown eyes gazing down at her in sympathy, and the touch of his hand.

"One of you guys want to see if you can scare up some

ice?" he asked over his shoulder, his eyes never leaving hers.

Sabrina reached up and felt the tender flesh at the top of her cheekbone. It was already beginning to swell.

"Joey practically nailed her right between the eyes."

"Did you check her pulse? Is she breathing okay?" Another of the group shouldered his way through the clutch of onlookers. "Maybe she needs CPR."

"Or mouth-to-mouth," one of the guys offered suggestively.

"She got hit with a football, Frankie. She didn't have a heart attack. She's still conscious." Tommy gave Sabrina a puzzled look. "At least I think she is."

Frankie laid two fingers against Sabrina's wrist briefly, then drew back. "Yeah, I guess you're right. Her pulse is okay."

"She's doing wonders for *my* pulse, that's for sure, eh, Buddy?" The speaker, a tall gangly fellow, elbowed one of his pals in the ribs.

"Knock it off, Goober," Tommy warned. Someone appeared with melting ice wrapped in a paper towel.

"Sorry. It's all I could find."

"Thanks, Ollie." Tommy took it from him and pressed it against the swelling. Sabrina gasped at the coldness. *Now* the pain was setting in. Tommy helped her to her feet. The other men were shuffling around nearby, watching the two of them as if they didn't know what to do with themselves.

"Everybody, this is Sabrina. Sabrina, these are the guys."

Sabrina tried to smile, but her cheek was really beginning to throb. The whole area around her eye felt tender and bruised. Drops of icy water dripped from the paper towel through her fingers and down her arm.

"This is Joey, and Mikey. Ollie and Buddy. Goober and Frankie."

Sabrina nodded at each of them in turn. They seemed pleasant enough though their names all swirled together in her mind. She knew she'd never remember them were she to meet them again.

As Tommy's buddies shuffled off, Sabrina started for the porch steps. She wanted to get inside and assess the damage. She wanted to get rid of the dripping paper towel and get a proper ice pack. Most of all, she wanted to get away from Tommy's presence, the concern she saw in his eyes, but he was right behind her and he reached past her to open the door.

"You don't have to come in. I'm fine."

"I was supposed to catch that pass."

"I, uh . . ." She couldn't think with him so near. Her fingers fluttered through the air as if they didn't know where to go. They landed on his tanned and muscled forearm.

Warning! Her internal system shouted. *Unidentified male has breached the neutral zone.*

"You're going to have quite a shiner."

Tommy's words barely penetrated the fog in her brain. She tried to remember why her hand was touching his arm.

"Could you, um, hmmm." She pretended her only intention was to reassure him by patting his arm as if he were a five-year-old. "I'll be fine."

Tommy didn't take the hint. Instead he followed her into the half bath near the kitchen. She lowered the sopping paper towel and stared at her reflection.

"Oh, no—look what you've done." Her eyes filled with tears. Well, her undamaged right eye filled with tears. Her left eye was nearly swollen shut, so the tears simply oozed out between the lids. "Look at me. I'm ruined."

Tommy regarded her intently. "Yep. I was right. Quite a shiner you got there. Better put some more ice on it. Got any aspirin?"

"Ice! Aspirin! You are missing the point. Look at me!"

"Yeah, I see. A black eye. Don't worry. The swelling will go down in a day or two. It'll only have that purplish-black hue for about a week or ten days."

"A week or ten days! School starts *tomorrow!*"

Sabrina pushed past him to the kitchen and the refrigerator. She dampened a towel and filled it with ice cubes. "I can't believe it. The first day of school and I'll show up looking like the bully on the playground beat me up, thanks to you." She sniffed and chanced a glance Tommy's way from beneath her lashes.

His attention was focused on Victoria, who was twining her body lovingly around his jeans-clad ankles. He bent down to rub her under the chin. Sabrina could hear the cat purring loudly at the attention. What did that cat see in Tommy Cameron, anyway? Maybe Victoria hadn't figured out that Tommy was responsible for her mistress's black eye. Or for Skid chasing her the other day. Maybe Victoria had short-term memory loss. Or maybe she'd already forgiven Tommy for his dog's behavior.

He picked up the cat and looked back at Sabrina. "Should I take you to the emergency room?"

"No. I'll be all right."

Sabrina looked at the purring cat and then at Tommy.

She thought about giving them both the look she'd perfected for use in her classes. Rumor had it that that particular look could freeze ice. It had never worked on Victoria. She doubted it would work on Tommy.

"I'm really sorry about the football. I'll make it up to you."

"How? I have to show up in front of my students tomorrow looking like this. Teachers aren't supposed to look like they just stepped out of a boxing ring. They're supposed to be stable and responsible and set a good example. What am I going to say? That I walked into a door?"

"What's wrong with the truth? You got hit by a football. They'll think you were playing. They'll think you're cool. Especially the guys. If they don't already, that is."

Something in his gaze disturbed her. She chose to ignore it and focused on arguing with him. "What's that supposed to mean?"

"It means I'd have counted my lucky stars if I had a teacher who looked like you when I was in high school. And if she played football on top of it, I'd have been pretty impressed."

Sabrina blushed at the compliment. "I'm sure my male students don't think of me that way, and the last thing I want to do is encourage them to."

Tommy lifted an eyebrow. "Oh, yeah? Well, you better think again. Play up the football thing for all it's worth. Tell them you went up to block a pass and got nailed with the ball."

"That would be lying," Sabrina pointed out.

"Fine. Tell them your obnoxious but sexy new neighbor got distracted when he saw you fussing over your roses and didn't catch the pass like he was supposed to. That's a much better story. And it's true."

Sabrina chose to ignore the message Tommy was quite obviously trying to send her. "I was *not* fussing over my roses. I was attempting to prune them."

"Whatever you were doing, it was distracting."

Sabrina's skin started to prickle in warning. Tommy Cameron was not going to get to her. He wasn't her type. She didn't even like him that much. He was pleasant enough, certainly—her neighbor—but nothing more.

"I'm sure your friends are waiting for you."

Tommy took the hint. He lowered Victoria to the floor, but then took a step closer to Sabrina. She watched him warily as he put a finger beneath her chin. "I'll make it up to you. I promise."

Then he was gone, and Sabrina was left to contemplate the various possibilities his parting words evoked and why even his lightest touch sent a shiver down her spine.

Chapter Five

The guys were tossing the football around as Tommy loped across the lawn.

"We still gonna play?" Goober Davies asked.

Tommy shrugged, took a cold soda from the cooler on the porch, popped the tab, and sat down on the top step. He wasn't much in the mood for a game of football anymore.

"Your girlfriend gonna be all right, Tommy boy?" Goober teased as he threw a perfect spiral to Mikey Muldoon.

Tommy frowned. "She's not my girlfriend." *Not yet, anyway. And at the rate I'm going, I probably don't stand a chance with her.*

He saw Goober wink at Mikey, and he heard Ollie Patterson's chuckle from where he lounged on the grass nearby.

"Could have fooled me," Joey Gianetti put in. He signaled Goober to go long and ran to the edge of the lawn where he neatly caught a pass. "See, Tom, that's how it's done. You got to keep your eye on the ball. Can't let no woman on the sidelines distract you."

"Ha, ha," Tommy responded without humor. He'd known all these guys since grade school. They'd grown up with each other, played sports together, helped each other through thick and thin. He had a history with them. But sometimes he wished they'd all just leave him alone. Like now.

Frankie Long, who was his closest friend, sat on the porch rail nearby, swung one leg back and forth, and sipped a soda. "She is sorta cute, Tom," he commented.

Tommy took a sip of root beer and offered up a non-committal grunt.

"Yeah, she's not bad-looking or anything," Ollie chimed in. " 'Cept she dresses sort of weird. Green overalls? And I never saw any shoes like those before."

"I believe those were gardening clogs," Tommy informed him. He grinned as he recalled Sabrina's outfit: Leaf-green coveralls, a yellow T-shirt, bright blue rubber clogs. She looked like she belonged in a garden. Like she was one of the brightly colored flowers.

"Oh, two days living next door to her, and you're already familiar with her wardrobe, huh?" Frankie leaned down and punched Tommy's shoulder.

"Knock it off," Tommy warned.

The other guys, sensing interesting conversation about to take place, gave up tossing the football and edged closer.

"Hey, maybe she'll fit into your five-year plan," Joey suggested. "She's got a job, right?"

Tommy nodded. "She's a teacher."

"And she owns her own place."

"Her grandmother left it to her."

"Good. Good. You always did go for the independent type." This came from Frankie.

"Yeah, and she's good-looking. Well, except for those shoes," Ollie added.

"Forget the shoes, Ollie. It's not like she wears them all the time."

"How's she kiss?" Goober wanted to know. "I saw you kissing her at the party the other night."

Tommy cleared his throat and stared Goober down. "None of your business."

"Okay. She's a good kisser," Goober told the others triumphantly. "Boys, I think we have a winner."

"Tommy's got a girlfriend. Tommy's got a girlfriend," Ollie teased.

"What are you? Six years old? Grow up." It was hard to be annoyed with Ollie, though. He was always so upbeat. "Besides, there's a problem."

"Problem?" The guys moved in closer as if they planned to put their heads together to solve Tommy's love life.

"*Problems,* actually."

Goober nudged Mikey and winked at Frankie. "You're talking to the experts. Fire away."

Tommy stretched out his legs and leaned back. "Are you forgetting we just gave her a black eye?"

"We?" Joey exclaimed. "We? Uh, Tommy, I think you're forgetting, you were the one who was supposed to catch that ball. It was a perfect pass. I should know. I threw it."

"Okay. *I* just gave her black eye. She's a little upset because school starts tomorrow. She's gonna look like she just went a round with Oscar de la Hoya."

"I'm sure you'll find a way to make it up to her." Frankie patted his shoulder.

Yeah, but how? Tommy wondered.

"She also met Skid, and she's not too crazy about him. Especially after he dug up one of her rosebushes."

At the mention of his name, Skid, who had been lying just inside the screen door, began to whine. Frankie got up and opened the door for him. The dog slathered Tommy's face with a slobbery pink tongue before making the rounds to the other guys, receiving their pats and ear-scratching as his due. "So keep him out of her roses. He'll grow on her," Goober said, as if he were an expert on pleasing women. "What else?"

Tommy thought for a moment. He hadn't made a very good impression on Sabrina thus far. First, he'd walked in on her private exercise session and then, Skid had chased her cat all over her house. When he kissed her at the party, she seemed to sort of like it. But then she disappeared. After Skid dug up her rosebush, she invited him to tea, but she'd acted uncomfortable the entire time he'd been in her house. If he wasn't mistaken, she'd glared at him when he picked up her cat. And now she was going to face the first day of the school year with a black eye because of him.

He looked around at the expectant faces of his friends. Might as well tell them the truth. "She may learn to like Skid eventually. But I'm not sure I'll ever convince her to like me."

Sabrina slept badly, mostly due to her attempts to keep her swollen eye under ice. When she dozed off she had odd dreams of Tommy and Skid chasing her while Tommy's circle of male friends looked on and applauded. She dreamt that Skid's pink tongue left a wet trail across her cheek, but she woke to discover it was merely a trickle of water from the ice pack dribbling across her skin to soak her pillow.

When her alarm went off she dragged herself to the bathroom, prepared for the worst. But she still gasped as she surveyed her damaged appearance. Her eye wasn't quite swollen shut, but it was puffy all the way around and had started to bruise in various shades of yellow and purple.

Perhaps she could just crawl back under the covers and hide for a week or so until she was presentable once again? Of course she knew she couldn't do that. Oglethorpe High awaited. Her new students would be anxious for their first assignment. She would have to face them like this and make the best of it whether she wanted to or not.

She donned her workout clothes and shoes, as she did every morning, for her thirty-minute power walk.

After a shower, she dressed in a buttercup yellow suit and matching sandals. Then she applied makeup with care, avoiding the bruised areas. She blew her hair dry and brushed it until it was shiny, then stepped back to survey her work. As usual, she'd tried to perfect her outward appearance, but now there was one glaring flaw. Since there was nothing she could do about it, she ate her breakfast of tea and yogurt while she scanned the newspaper. Victoria wandered in to pick at the food in her dish. She washed herself briefly, then sat and fixed Sabrina with her unblinking blue eyes until Sabrina couldn't stand it any longer.

"What?" she asked the cat. "What do you want from me? I can't bring Grandma Mamie back. I know you loved her. So did I. But it's been over two years now, so you better get used to it."

In answer Victoria jumped to the window ledge and stared pointedly at the house next door. Tommy's house.

"Oh, so it's *him* you want," Sabrina said in disgust as she threw the empty yogurt container in the trash and rinsed out her teacup. "Well, I've got news for you. That was his dog that chased you around the other day. And he's the reason I've got this black eye. So I don't care how much you like it when he rubs you under the chin, you are to stay away from him. Do you understand?"

Victoria yawned and continued to stare out the window, her back to Sabrina.

"I have to stop talking to you, Victoria. You're a lousy conversationalist. Plus, you know I'm right. That Tommy Cameron, he's a—a bad influence, that's what he is. He lives next door and we can be neighborly, of course, but that's as far as it goes."

Victoria looked over her shoulder and Sabrina could swear the cat's gaze swerved to the clock on the wall before she turned back to the window.

Sabrina took the hint.

"Wow, Miss Talbott, what happened to you?" In her first-period class, Eddie Morton looked in awe at her black eye.

"Somebody beat you up, Miss Talbott?" Liz Keller asked.

"Car wreck," Dan Simpson stated emphatically. "Right, Miss Talbott?"

She shook her head. She'd decided to take Tommy's advice and just tell the truth. "It was a football," she began.

"Wow! You play football, Teach?" Eddie asked. "What position?"

"No, I wasn't—"

"Running back. Look at the way she's built," one of the other guys put in.

"Wide receiver, maybe. Or a kicker," someone else commented.

"Oh, come on. She'd get nailed as a wide receiver."

"She did get nailed." The speaker indicated Sabrina's black eye. "That's the point."

"What about it, Miss Talbott? Were you going out for a pass? Somebody tried to intercept. You took an elbow to the eye?"

"No, I didn't see the ball coming—"

"Oh, man, you got to keep your eye on the ball. That's what coach always tells us. Keep your eye on the ball."

"That's baseball, Eddie. Not football."

"Yeah, well, same principles apply."

"Not if you're blocking—"

"Boys, please. There was a football game. I got hit with the ball because I wasn't paying attention. And I now have a black eye. Let that be a lesson to you."

"Yeah, like I said, you gotta keep your eye on the ball," Eddie agreed.

"She's talking about paying attention. In class," Liz informed him. "Right, Miss Talbott?" Liz beamed at her.

"You're such a teacher's pet," Eddie hissed.

Sabrina picked up her roll book. Five minutes into her first class on the first day of school and already she'd lost control.

And it was all Tommy Cameron's fault.

Chapter Six

She'd been fighting all day, it seemed, to get her students to show some interest in something, anything, other than her black eye. Each class started the same way, with exclamations and questions and an inevitable discussion of her football prowess. By lunchtime she was sure she had become a legend in her own time. Tommy was right. Many of the students thought she was "cool" due to her football injury. Even the captain of the football team gave her a thumbs-up as he passed her in the hallway. Sabrina knew she shouldn't be enjoying the unaccustomed attention, but she was.

Her best friend, Elaine Peters, who taught math, insisted on details during the break. Sabrina found herself reluctant to disillusion anyone with a blatant and, frankly, boring version of the truth. She managed to fill in the blanks without telling any lies over lunch in the teacher's lounge so even Elaine was impressed.

"That's so unlike you. Getting involved in a team sport like football. Especially with a bunch of guys you hardly know."

Sabrina carefully drizzled the last of the Italian vinaigrette over her salad. "What's that supposed to mean?"

"Nothing, except you're not a joiner. You don't like to be *jostled*." Elaine leaned forward for added emphasis.

"It was just Tommy, my neighbor, and a few of his friends. And I didn't get jostled very much." Even to Sabrina's own ears, she sounded defensive. And the only time she'd been touched had been by Tommy when he caught her, and later when he'd stroked his finger under her chin. Sabrina shivered and changed the subject hoping Elaine wouldn't notice.

By the time she arrived home that afternoon, she had a plan firmly in place. She would banish all thoughts of her new neighbor from her mind. She would extend the olive branch of friendship and neighborliness to Tommy Cameron should their paths cross again. Period.

"Ahhh!" she cried as she came up the walk where an impressive pile of dirt and mulch greeted her. She picked up the bedraggled rosebush Tommy had planted the day before yesterday. The one tiny bud, with a hint of pink petals, was crushed and trampled. First Mamie's prize-winner, and now its replacement!

Sabrina marched across her lawn and her neighbor's and pounded on Tommy's front door. Not that he'd be home, of course. Not at 3:30 in the afternoon. He probably finished his workday at five like everyone else and wouldn't arrive home until evening.

Still, it felt good to pound on the door and vent her

frustration. The nerve of that dog. No—it wasn't the dog's fault. The nerve of the dog's owner. If Tommy didn't do something about Skid, she was going to file a complaint. She'd notify animal control. She'd—

"Hi." A pair of sleepy brown eyes greeted her from behind the screen door. Tommy held a mug of what smelled like coffee in one hand. "You're out of school already, huh? I didn't think you'd be home so early. Nice outfit. How's the eye?"

"Early? Early! It's almost four o'clock! Look what your dog did! What you allowed him to do. Again!"

Mindful of the thorns, Sabrina shook the damaged plant. Globules of damp earth spattered onto the porch and onto her skirt and shoes. "Where is that dog of yours? If you don't teach him to behave. . . ." She shook the rosebush again in menace.

The screen door burst open and Skid bounded out. He jumped up on Sabrina and lunged for the rosebush, which she dropped with a cry of outrage. More dirt dribbled down the front of her suit. Skid grabbed the bush between his teeth and dashed around the yard in a circle before returning to the porch. Apparently immune to the thorns, he gave it one last shake, sending more dirt particles flying in Sabrina's direction before dropping it at her feet.

He sat down in front of her and gave her his goofy grin as if quite pleased by his performance.

"Oh! Oh! Just look at this!" Sabrina brushed ineffectually at the dirt on her skirt, smearing it further.

Tommy opened the screen door. "Skid. Come here."

With a regretful glance in Sabrina's direction, the dog complied. Tommy closed the inner door as well as the screen and joined Sabrina on the porch, mug in hand.

A glance up confirmed her worst fears. Even though he

was trying not to show it, Tommy was amused by her. Somehow, that infuriated her more than anything his dog had done so far. More than anything *he* had done so far.

"Just forget it," she said. She kicked the damaged rosebush out of the way, not caring any longer if her pretty yellow sandals were ruined. Her outfit was a mess.

She stomped off the porch.

"Hey, wait a minute," Tommy called.

Sabrina ignored him. Animal control office, she thought. The town council. Her state representative. The governor. . . .

"Sabrina!" Tommy caught her elbow, effectively halting her. She jerked away from him, accidentally hitting his coffee mug. Warm brown liquid leapt from the cup to soak the top of her suit. The effect was now complete. Her beautiful buttercup yellow outfit was ruined.

She felt her bottom lip begin to tremble. In her frustration, she knew herself to be dangerously close to tears. Over what? A black eye? Her clothes? An uncontrollable dog? Another rosebush lost? Ever since Tommy Cameron moved in next door her previously perfect, serene existence seemed headed for disaster.

"I said forget it." She started toward her house again. Tears leaked beneath her lashes. She must be under more stress than she realized. She never lost control like this.

"Sabrina."

She hadn't taken two steps before she found herself enfolded in Tommy's embrace. His coffee mug was gone. His arms were around her. One of his hands cradled the back of her head. Her face was buried in the solid comfort of his T-shirt-covered chest. He smelled like he'd just gotten out of the shower and donned clean clothes. Evidently, Skid hadn't gotten hold of him yet today. As quickly as they'd begun, the tears stopped.

She should step back. There was no reason to continue standing here letting him hold her. She didn't need his comfort. She didn't need anything from him. Except for his dog to leave her garden alone. Except for him to leave her alone too. Her feet, however, refused to move.

"Better now?" Tommy asked a moment later.

Sabrina nodded. Up and down against his chest. The scents of fabric softener and pure male surrounded her. She felt his hand smoothing the hair along the back of her head like he was petting her. If she stayed where she was, she'd probably start to purr just like Victoria had when Tommy held her.

"How about this?" Tommy's voice washed over her. "You go change your clothes. We'll go down to the garden center. I'll buy you two new rosebushes to replace the one Skid dug up."

She straightened away from him. "Why? So you can laugh at me some more?"

"I wasn't laughing at you."

Sabrina's eyebrow went up in an expression of disbelief.

"It's just that every time I see you, you look so perfect. I think you need your feathers ruffled every once in awhile." As if to make his point he messed up the hair on top of her head in an affectionate gesture.

Sabrina shook her head. "It won't matter how many rosebushes you buy, Tom . . . uh, Tommy. He'll just keep digging them up. You have to do something about his behavior."

"Like what?"

They started walking toward her front porch. "Like train

him. Teach him how to behave. You need to learn how to control him."

"Okay. Maybe you're right. But first, let me make this up to you. Come with me and pick out new rosebushes."

At her front door, Sabrina paused. There was nothing she liked more than a trip to the garden center. She'd find the biggest, most exotic, most expensive rosebushes she could. And Tommy Cameron would pay. She'd make sure of it.

Of course, it really was much too late in the year to be planting rosebushes. They'd probably freeze in the first cold snap, although she'd heard of certain varieties designed specifically to bloom in the fall. Maybe Gill's Greenhouse would have some.

Clearly, Tommy wanted to make up for Skid's faux pas.

She gestured down at her outfit. "If the dry cleaners can't get this out. . . ."

"I'll buy you a new one."

Sabrina opened her door. "I'll be ready in twenty minutes." She closed the door. For the life of her she couldn't figure out why Tommy was smiling.

She changed clothes quickly and swallowed one of the new allergy pills her doctor had prescribed. Nothing triggered a fit of sneezing and sniffles like a trip to the greenhouse. All those plants in an enclosed space wreaked havoc with her sinuses.

They spent what was left of the afternoon scouring each of Oglethorpe's garden centers and greenhouses for rosebushes. Ordinarily Sabrina shopped at the same place for all of her gardening needs. Perversely, she saved that place for last, unwilling to admit that the postponement was so she could prolong her time with Tommy.

He drove an old Jeep from which he'd removed the collapsible top and sides. Strapped into the seat next to him, Sabrina felt an odd sense of freedom as the sun poured down on them and the wind blew her hair in all directions.

It was an impractical vehicle, she reminded herself. What happened when it rained? Or snowed? Surely the vinyl covering was no defense against inclement weather.

But on a perfect late summer day, they had no need of such protection. Her gaze wandered more than once to Tommy's hands curved around the steering wheel or the gearshift. She watched the way he handled the accelerator and clutch, shifting smoothly from long practice.

He filled up the Jeep the way he seemed to fill up every place he happened to occupy. His long legs and muscular thighs were hidden beneath a layer of faded denim. The tanned length of his arm from elbow to fingertips fascinated her. She wished the muscles of his chest and shoulders weren't covered by a dark blue T-shirt.

Their gazes collided, then connected when he caught her looking at him. What red-blooded female wouldn't do the same? Tommy was attractive in his own way. Sure he could use a haircut. What would he looked like all spiffed up in a navy blue pinstriped suit? A starched white dress shirt with a button-down collar and a Brooks Brothers tie? He wouldn't look like Tommy anymore, that was for sure. He'd look like—she was aghast at the possibility—Mr. Perfect!

No. No way. No how. Tommy Cameron was never going to turn into her Mr. Perfect. Not in a million years. Not even if she thought for a second she might want him to. Which she certainly did not!

She crossed her arms over her chest and purposely stared in the opposite direction.

If Sabrina gave him that appraising once-over one more time, Tommy thought, he'd have to pull over and pick up where they left off the other night.

Her body language might be saying no, but her eyes were saying yes. Yes. Yes!

Sabrina Talbott could be as prickly as a porcupine, but underneath the nettles, as he'd already discovered, she was warm and soft. He bet if he could navigate past those thorns, he'd find out all kinds of good things about her.

When she'd dropped into his arms yesterday, that odd kind of possessive feeling he'd had about her had been further reinforced. He wasn't sure he *wanted* to feel that feeling, but still, he hadn't liked the other guys joking about her.

Holding her next to him, swaying to the music the other night, contentment had washed over him. She smelled good. And she felt good. She felt . . . right in his arms. And he had liked having her there. Almost too much.

And that kiss. Wow! Oh, he'd sensed her hesitation at first. But it hadn't lasted long. And the kissing itself hadn't lasted long enough as far as he was concerned.

Until a couple of years ago, Tommy had liked his life just fine. He liked his work designing computer software. He liked setting his own schedule. His friends were around to keep him company whenever he needed them. If he wanted to have a party, there was no reason he couldn't. So what if he was usually alone the rest of the time? That was just fine too, he assured himself.

But the year he turned twenty-seven he took a hard look at his life. After years of dating, he had no steady companion. He was sick of apartment life. He looked forward to visits from his nieces and nephews.

That's when he came up with the five-year plan. His friends thought he was crazy. Most of them were still enjoying the bachelor life. But he knew what he wanted. He'd become well enough established in his business that he could afford to buy a home of his own, and the McDermott place was exactly what he'd envisioned: an older home with some character on a street lined with trees and sidewalks where children played and rode bikes. So that was one thing crossed off his list.

Now all he had to do was find someone special with whom to share it. And then a family would follow. A big family like his own, he hoped. He tried to picture Sabrina as the mother of his children. Even after only a couple of days of knowing her, that part was easy. Convincing Sabrina to go along with his plan, that part might be a bit more difficult.

A woman like Sabrina could be a lot of work. Already he was making his second rose-buying expedition in less than two days.

He thought about spending lots more time with Sabrina. Sabrina with her roses-and-cream skin, and those sparkly tanzanite-colored eyes and silky dark hair.

Sabrina with her constant criticism of his dog's behavior. Her perfect house with its polished antiques and collection of teapots.

Sabrina smiling at his lame jokes about crumpets.

Sabrina getting a black eye because of the football he was supposed to catch.

Abruptly, he slammed on the brakes, figuratively and literally as he almost missed the turnoff for the last garden center. Sabrina shot him a curious glance which he ignored as he parked.

Okay, so he admitted to himself it was sort of fun reaching out to ruffle Sabrina's feathers. Or, in this case, quills.

He just wanted to make sure he could get his hand back intact afterward.

Chapter Seven

Sabrina took her time choosing her plants, even though this late in the season there weren't that many left and she'd spotted the two she wanted almost immediately.

Tommy Cameron, she had ascertained, was long on patience. Could it be he had nothing better to do on a Monday afternoon? Like work? And if not, why not?

Because Tommy was a free spirit, that's why. He did as he pleased, operated on his own schedule. He answered to no one. So if he wanted to spend the afternoon watching his neighbor peruse rosebushes at one garden center after another, there was no one to tell him he couldn't or shouldn't.

Sabrina felt a tiny spark of envy for Tommy's apparent freedom as he paid for her purchases. Already she was thinking of her own schedule, her classes, the papers she had to assign, the English department staff meeting tomorrow afternoon.

"How about stopping for something to eat?" Tommy asked after he stowed the bushes in the back of the Jeep.

"That would be lovely, but I, uh. . . ." Sabrina hesitated. She was starving after her yogurt breakfast and salad lunch. But sharing a meal with Tommy? That would be too much like a date. No. He was so not her type.

"Red's is right up here," Tommy said. He slowed and turned into the parking lot. "Best barbecued ribs and fried chicken in town."

Red's, Sabrina thought with trepidation. She knew it was the kind of place where a largely male crowd gathered to play pool or watch sports events on big-screen TVs. Not the kind of place where she would fit in.

He parked and gave her that grin, his eyes full of mischief. "Come on. I'll buy you a root beer."

Sabrina shook her head. "I don't think so."

"Oh, come on now." Tommy poked her gently in the ribs. "What do you like to drink? Mineral water? Iced tea? Shirley Temples?" His finger wiggled a little more with each possibility. He was tickling her! Sabrina did her best not to giggle.

"Banana milk shakes?"

"No!"

"Strawberry smoothies? Grape juice?"

"No!" Sabrina decided the best defense was a good offense. She launched herself at Tommy, managing to tickle him under the arm before he laughed and twisted away.

Encouraged by her success, Sabrina focused on finding other openings. While she searched for Tommy's weak spot, she had to keep him from tickling her too.

"Orange soda? V-8? Iced coffee?"

Intent on besting him at this tickling game, Sabrina didn't answer. While he squirmed beneath her, dodging her attempts to get her hands on him, Tommy slunk down sideways in his seat until she was on top of him. Being with Tommy caused her to do all sorts of wild and crazy things. Such inappropriate behavior! She'd forgotten herself. All because she'd been having . . . fun?

Sabrina's cheeks turned pink. What if one of her students saw her? Or a student's parents? Or Principal Strickland? She struggled to return to an upright position before she lost the tight grip she always had on her self-control and did something really stupid. Like kissed him. Seizing the opening she'd left him, Tommy dug his knuckles into her ribs just as she turned away. Unprepared for his sudden move, she jerked at his touch. Due to her already precarious position, she slipped. Her mouth connected with the steering wheel and a stinging pain shot through her lip.

"Owwwww," she wailed as she righted herself and covered her mouth with her hand. She pulled down the visor, but there was no vanity mirror in Tommy's Jeep.

Tommy rearranged himself to a sitting position in his seat and leaned toward her. "Let me see." In a repeat of the previous day, he cupped her hand in his and drew it away from her face. "Oh, it's not too bad. Just a little bit of blood. You'll be okay."

"Blood!" Sabrina tentatively ran her tongue around the injured area. Tommy produced a crumpled but clean white handkerchief from his jeans pocket and handed it to her. She pressed it to the injured area and gasped at the sting. Her lip throbbed.

She fumbled in her purse for a compact. Lowering the handkerchief, she examined her tiny reflection. "Lovely. Just lovely," she murmured. The swelling had gone down a little bit around her left eye, but the purple and yellow bruising had really taken hold. And now the right side of her mouth was beginning to swell as the cut continued to ooze.

She remembered her earlier discussion with Victoria. Tommy Cameron was a bad influence.

Tommy straightened in his own seat and shoved his fingers through his disheveled hair with a quick glance in the rearview mirror.

He opened his door, then closed it and looked at her. "Still want to go in? Or would you rather go home?"

Sabrina stopped staring at her colorful face. "Frankly, I've been wondering what you were thinking. Why would you even want to be seen with someone who looks as bad as I do?"

Tommy shrugged. "I hadn't really thought about it. I try not to judge people based on superficialities like physical appearance."

Superficialities? A seven-syllable word dropped into casual conversation? Was he trying to impress her with his vocabulary? Perhaps there was more to Tommy Cameron than met the eye. He might not judge others on their physical appearance, but plenty of other people did. Especially men. It would serve him right to show up in a place like Red's with someone looking as decidedly unattractive as she did at the moment.

They were inside the restaurant before she remembered she'd been debating the wisdom of dining with him.

She'd been by Red's a hundred times or more, but she'd never been inside, since it wasn't the type of place she frequented on a weeknight. Or any other occasion for that matter. But since Tommy had moved in next door, her life had ceased to be normal. Predictable. Stable. Boring.

Stop it, she internally hissed at her subconscious, which insisted on putting words in her head. Just because she liked regular schedules, daily rituals, and rosebushes that stayed where she planted them, that did not make her *boring!*

"Hey, Tommy boy!" From behind the bar the owner called an enthusiastic greeting in their direction.

Tommy raised a hand. "Yo, Red! What's up?" he called back.

Several of the other male patrons who were gathered along the bar turned around to greet Tommy as well. Their curious eyes gave her a friendly, assessing once-over. Sabrina fought the urge to run a hand over her hair to make sure it didn't look too windblown. Like it would matter with her face looking as it did. She pressed Tommy's handkerchief to her lip. At least the bleeding seemed to have stopped.

Eventually, the men refocused their attention on the baseball game playing on a television set high at one end of the long polished surface.

She followed Tommy to a table where to her surprise he pulled out her chair. A waitress appeared, grinned at Tommy, and handed them menus.

"Hey, Tommy boy. What's happening? Heard you had quite a party the other night."

"Yep. Moved into my new place."

"So I heard. Frankie and Buddy were in here Saturday around noon still feeling the effects." She chuckled. "What can I get you to drink?"

"I'll have a root beer," Tommy said.

When in Rome, Sabrina thought. "I'll have a root beer too."

He nodded. "And could you bring us a glass of ice too, Sandy?"

"Sure thing." The waitress left.

Sabrina studied her menu. Tommy didn't even open his. Red's offered hearty fare: ribs, fried chicken, country-fried steak, hamburgers. All served with french fries or mashed potatoes and cole slaw. She scanned the menu for something healthier, like grilled chicken or a salad. Surely Red's had a salad menu.

"You might as well order the ribs. You'll be sorry if you don't."

Sabrina glanced up. Tommy had tipped his chair back on two legs and was rocking back and forth, steadying himself with one hand on the edge of the table.

"Oh, wait a minute. I'll bet you don't eat ribs," he said.

Sabrina closed her menu. "What makes you think I don't eat ribs?"

Tommy shrugged and glanced over at the television for a minute before fixing her with his smiling brown eyes again. "I just figured they'd be too messy for you. Or too high a calorie count."

"I'm not afraid of getting messy," Sabrina told him defiantly. "I'm not afraid of calories."

"Oh. Okay. My mistake." He set his chair back on the floor properly just as the waitress arrived with their drinks and a glass filled with ice.

"You two ready to order?"

"I'll have ribs, Sandy," Tommy answered. "With fries."

Sandy scribbled on her pad. "How 'bout you, hon?"

Sabrina moved her closed menu aside, keeping her gaze locked with Tommy's. "The same." There. That ought to fix him, Sabrina thought. Afraid to get messy! How dare he make such an assumption. She'd been messy plenty of times. Especially in the past couple of days, after being hit in the head with a football. All he had to do was look at her black eye and her split lip. Now *there* was a real mess.

She'd show Tommy she wasn't afraid to eat ribs dripping with barbeque sauce, fries covered with salt, or cole slaw drowned in mayonnaise. Sabrina's mouth watered.

"Okay, Tommy boy, I'll put this right in for you." Sandy moved on to the next table.

"Doesn't that bother you?"

Tommy arranged several ice cubes in the middle of his handkerchief and wound the cloth around them before handing the bundle to Sabrina. Then he tipped his chair back again and rocked.

"What?"

"People calling you 'Tommy boy'? You're not a child. At least not physically." Sabrina pressed the makeshift ice pack against her lip.

A slow smile spread across Tommy's features. He set his chair back down and took a drink of his root beer. "Should it?"

"Should what?" Sabrina had been distracted by that slow smile. And the way he licked his lips after he swallowed. She'd watched his Adam's apple bob above the neckline of his T-shirt.

"Bother me that people call me 'Tommy boy'?"

Sabrina snapped her gaze back to his, but her focus wavered. A layer of fuzz suddenly wrapped itself around her brain courtesy of her new allergy medication.

"I'm sorry. What was the question?"

Tommy snorted. "Forget it."

"Oh, I remember. 'Tommy boy.' I meant, well, look at you." Sabrina gestured with her hand. "You're a mature, uh, that is, you're an adult. And Tommy is more of a nick-name for a . . . child?"

Tommy frowned. Sabrina felt herself losing ground. She took a sip of her drink to counteract the dryness in her mouth. She experienced instant numbing in her extremities, followed by a tingling sensation. Never before had an al-lergy medication made her feel this way.

"And what should people call me? 'Thomas?' "

His lips curled when he said it.

Sabrina couldn't remember why she'd brought this up. She couldn't remember much of anything at the moment.

"Maybe not 'Thomas.' That's a bit too formal for some-one like you." She brightened. "What about 'Tom?' "

Tommy shrugged. "I don't mind 'Tom' so much. But everyone's called me Tommy for as long as I can remem-ber. What about you? Don't you have a nickname?"

"For Sabrina?" She shook her head.

"What about Bree?"

"No one ever called me that. I've always been Sabrina." Except for her stepfather Ted occasionally calling her "Sweet Pea," she'd never had a nickname.

Tommy leaned across the table. "If I called you Bree, would you come?"

Sabrina surprised herself. She didn't blush. She grinned and leaned toward Tommy. "You never know. I just might."

Tommy lifted his glass in a toast and Sabrina followed suit. The glasses clinked and Sabrina was too pleased with herself to wonder why Tommy had such a triumphant gleam in his eye.

Chapter Eight

S andy set plates piled high with ribs, fries, and cole slaw
down in front of them.

Sabrina giggled. "I think my new allergy pills are making
made me a little goofy."

"What are you allergic to? Me?" Tommy asked.

She hoped he didn't expect an answer to that. Tommy
triggered an entirely different reaction in her than ragweed
and pollen. She could imagine Dr. Sever looking up her
complaint in one of his medical manuals. Diagnosis: Attraction to unsuitable male. Cure: None known.

When she didn't reply, Tommy pulled a rib off the slab
on his plate and began to eat. In minutes, his fingers were
sticky with barbecue sauce. He tore paper towels off the
roll on the table and wiped his hands and mouth. Then he
drowned his french fries in ketchup.

Sabrina wondered if there was any way to eat her ribs

without making such a mess. With her fork, she speared a french fry and took a bite. Could she possibly use her utensils and just cut the meat off the bones?

Tommy stopped eating and watched her. She could almost feel him gauge her hesitancy, ready to laugh at her unwillingness to get her fingers sticky.

Sandy returned with another round of drinks. *Thank goodness,* Sabrina thought. She took a fortifying swallow, set her glass back down, and tore into her ribs just as Tommy had. It wasn't so bad, she told herself, as the sauce oozed between her fingers and under her nails. She ate delicately, mindful of her swollen lip.

She managed to finish about half of the food on her plate and then fussed with the paper towel and the tiny wet wipe Sandy had left when she brought the check.

Sabrina knew she was a mess, but she didn't really care. She felt lighthearted and happy. In fact, she had the feeling that nothing was going to bother her for the rest of the evening.

"You missed some," Tommy said after she'd cleaned up as best she could.

"Where?"

"Right there." He took the dirty wet wipe from her and dabbed at the uninjured corner of her mouth. His fingers were so close to her lips she could flick her tongue out and lick them. If she wanted to. Which she certainly did not.

Except why was he looking at her like that? And why did her cheek feel all warm where he'd touched it? She could drown in the heat of those brown eyes if she wasn't careful.

"Maybe I'll just go to the ladies room." She stood and put her hand on the table to steady herself. She negotiated her way to the rest room and back without mishap.

"You want to take this home?" Tommy asked when she returned, gesturing at her half rack of ribs, the majority of fries which remained on her plate, and the cole slaw she'd hardly made a dent in.

She shook her head. "No, thanks."

"Mind if I do?"

Inwardly Sabrina recoiled at the thought of any human, even Tommy, eating cold french fries and ribs congealed with sauce. "Help yourself."

Tommy already had a styrofoam container open and ready on the table. Sandy must have brought it while she was in the rest room. He scraped the remains of her meal along with the few scraps left from his into it. On second thought, maybe Tommy needed the leftovers. Maybe money was tight at the moment. He drove an old vehicle. He'd just relocated. He'd had to spend money to replace her rosebushes. She felt a twinge of sympathy for him.

"I knew there was a reason Skid liked you," he said, as he closed the lid on the container.

"S-Skid?"

Tommy dropped a generous tip on the table, picked up the leftovers, and escorted Sabrina to the door. "Are you kidding? Skid loves ribs and cold french fries."

On the way home, she rested her head back against the seat as the cool evening air teased her face.

Sabrina felt deliciously light-headed as Tommy helped her out of the Jeep and walked her to her door.

"It's too bad, you know," she told him as they gained the porch.

"What's too bad?"

Sabrina dug in her bag for her keys. "It's too bad because you're a nice guy."

"And that's bad?"

"You're sort of irresponsible. Especially with that dog of yours."

"Here, let me." Tommy took the keys from her and fit the door key into the lock. Sabrina swayed against him and he put an arm around her.

She turned her face into his chest. "Hmmmm. And you smell good too. It's too bad you're so much fun."

"Okay, then." Tommy guided her over the threshold. "Bree, honey, maybe you ought to check the dosage on those allergy pills."

Victoria came gracefully toward them, her fluffy tail standing up like a straight arrow. She halted several feet away and gazed up at Sabrina with an expression of disgust.

Sabrina looked at the cat. "It's okay, Victoria. It's just Tommy. He's a bad influence just like I told you. And he's not my type. Look." She pointed to her lip and then she started to giggle and couldn't stop.

Tommy chose that moment to extricate himself. He ruffled the hair on top of her head. "Go to bed, Sabrina." He backed toward the door. "And hey, for what it's worth, I'm sorry about your lip."

Sabrina took a couple of steps toward him. "Okay, Tommy. Thanks for the roses. And the ribs."

Tommy unloaded the rosebushes and set them next to the walk. Tomorrow he'd plant them. And he wouldn't let Skid get anywhere near them.

Maybe Sabrina was right about one thing. He was definitely not her type. And she probably wasn't his. But irresponsible? Just because of Skid? Hadn't he replaced her rosebushes? Not once, but twice. Hadn't he apologized for his dog's wayward behavior? What more did she want?

And why did he care what his uptight, tea-drinking,

prissy neighbor thought of him anyway? *Because you like her,* his subconscious whispered back. Tommy chose to ignore it.

And what was wrong with his name? Tommy. Everybody called him Tommy. Tommy-boy. Good-time Tommy. What was so terrible about that? Plenty of people were called Tommy. And Sabrina wasn't getting all over their cases for it.

Tommy headed for his house. He had to let Skid out. The poor mongrel had been cooped up most of the day. This time, he'd make sure Skid was on a leash. *Irresponsible, my eye,* he thought, glancing back at Sabrina's porch.

For a moment there at Red's, he'd seen her actually relax a little. Take a chance. Lighten up. Have some fun. Even though her allergy medication seemed to have a rather odd effect on her, the only part of her that truly relaxed was her tongue. And he didn't particularly care for the words that had just come dripping off it. Good thing he wasn't her type. Otherwise, he might be really annoyed with her.

Sabrina struggled out of her car and up the walk the next afternoon, her bag nearly dragging on the ground. The headache she'd woken up with insisted on poking her behind the eyes every time she moved. Due to her colorful eye, hardly anyone noticed her split lip. The staff meeting had been sheer torture. Her still queasy stomach was even rejecting the idea of hot tea.

She stopped halfway up the walk when she saw Tommy and Skid coming toward her. Confused, she watched the two of them, the dog loping along next to Tommy's easy, long-legged stride.

"Hi, there." Tommy and Skid stopped a couple of feet away. Sabrina's mouth dropped open. She turned her gaze to her garden. The two rosebushes had been planted side by side. The buds on one were almost ready to burst open. She swung her gaze back to Tommy, and then to Skid, who offered her his usual goofy grin.

She set her heavy bag down to rub her aching temple. "What's going on?"

"Nothing. Why?"

She gestured at the rosebushes and then back at Skid. "My rosebushes are still in the ground. Your dog's on a leash. Have I just stepped into an alternate universe?"

Tommy chuckled. Skid's grin appeared to widen in appreciation of her feeble attempt at humor.

"I have to sit down." Sabrina made it to the porch steps before she crumpled. Her empty stomach heaved. Her head pounded.

"Hey. You don't look so good." Tommy followed and stopped a short distance away, restraining Skid when he started to lunge for her.

"Believe me. I don't feel so good."

"Maybe you're allergic to your allergy pills, huh? You know what you need?"

Sabrina eyed him warily. "Please don't say tea."

Tommy shook his head. "A couple of slices of cheese pizza with extra cheese."

"Ugh. Tommy, no." Sabrina held up her hand to stop him as her stomach pitched and churned.

"Salt. Fat. Carbs. It'll cure what ails you. And then you can go to class with me and Skid."

"What class?" Sabrina gasped.

"Obedience class. I took your suggestion. It starts tonight."

"Why do I have to go? I'm not the one misbehaving."

"Oh, well, you don't have to. I thought maybe you'd

want to. Since you kind of have a vested interest in his success." He glanced meaningfully at the still intact rosebushes.

"Oh, Tommy, I don't know." The last thing Sabrina felt like doing was attending a dog obedience class. With a dog that wasn't hers. A dog she wasn't particularly fond of at the moment.

Skid chose that moment to whine pitifully. He gave a short mournful bark and fixed her with pleading brown eyes.

"Go change your clothes. I'll bring the pizza over as soon as it arrives."

Two hours later, dressed in slacks and a matching short-sleeved blouse in a soft shade of pink, Sabrina watched as the trainer instructed the dog obedience class.

Skid turned out to be one of the brighter dogs in the group, and proved to be a better listener than many of his peers. Much of the first session was devoted to simple instructions, such as types of leashes and how to divert a dog's attention from undesirable pursuits.

Then the instructor had the owners free their dogs and, one by one, the owners called them to come.

Not all the dogs came when they were called, but Skid responded well to his master's encouraging, urgent tone. Skid had been avidly sniffing a young poodle, but Tommy somehow convinced the dog he had something much more interesting.

Only Sabrina saw Tommy reach into his pocket and slip the dog a treat after he snapped the leash on Skid's collar. Skid gazed up at Tommy affectionately, and Tommy rubbed him behind the ears while the other owners tried the calling technique.

Sabrina felt a twinge of regret for her behavior from the

moment she'd met Tommy. He was making an effort to train Skid just as she'd suggested. The instructor mentioned several times how important praise was in the training process.

She would try to be less critical of Tommy. And Skid.

When the class ended, the two of them strolled over to Sabrina. *A boy and his dog,* she thought. Tommy's grin was a mile wide. Skid's only a bit less so. *Praise,* she reminded herself. *Positive reinforcement.* She applauded them both. "You guys were wonderful!"

Skid lunged, but Tommy's grip on the leash kept him from pouncing on Sabrina. She leaned forward to rub him behind the ears as Tommy had. "Good boy. You're such a good boy, aren't you?" Skid moaned in ecstasy.

"What about me?" Tommy asked.

She glanced up. "What about you? Want me to rub you behind the ears?"

"That's not exactly what I had in mind, no."

Sabrina stood on tiptoe and kissed Tommy's cheek. "Ouch." She'd forgotten about her swollen lip. "Good boy, Tommy."

Tommy tickled her as they started toward the car. "How about some ice cream?"

Sabrina put her hands over her stomach. She'd already consumed several slices of pizza, and Tommy had been kind enough not to gloat when his remedy for her headache and queasy stomach had worked.

"Ice cream? No way. I can't eat ice cream. Not after that pizza. And those ribs last night."

"Aw, come on. I ate your crumpet, Miss Muffett."

"You can stop for ice cream if you want. But I'm not having any."

"Suit yourself."

Tommy drove to the nearby Frosty Freeze. "Sure you don't want anything?"

Yes! Her taste buds screamed. *A hot fudge sundae with extra hot fudge, whipped cream, and nuts!* "No, thanks."

She was almost certain she heard Tommy say something under his breath as he closed his door. It sounded like "liar."

From the backseat, Skid gave a sharp bark at Tommy's desertion. "It's okay, Skid." She rubbed him behind the ears. "He'll be right back."

Sure enough, Tommy returned, with two containers. "I told you I didn't want any!" she scolded.

"It's not for you. It's for him."

He set the Styrofoam cup filled with plain vanilla soft serve in the back of the Jeep. Skid settled down and began noisily lapping it up.

Tommy got into his seat and held the other container out to her. "Sure you don't want some?" He waved it under her nose. "Hot fudge. Nuts. Whipped cream."

Sabrina's taste buds groaned in deprivation. "Maybe just a bite. A little one."

Tommy held the spoon weighted with ice cream and toppings out to her. Sabrina took the offered bite and groaned in delight.

"Good?"

"Heavens, yes!"

"Want some more."

"No." She shook her head adamantly.

"Come on. One more bite."

"Okay. Just one more."

It was hard to say who ate more of Tommy's sundae. He scraped the last bits of ice cream from the bottom of the cup and held the spoon out to her. She shook her head, this time meaning it. "No. Finish it. I'm satisfied."

"Really? So how was it? Better than ribs and allergy pills?"

"Let's put it this way," Sabrina replied. "Ice cream and hot fudge causes an entirely different chemical reaction."

And so does being with you. She pushed that thought away. She gazed around, looking anywhere but at Tommy. Mr. Perfect had to be out there.

Somewhere.

Chapter Nine

"**S**o you think I'm irresponsible, huh?"

Tommy's question took Sabrina by surprise, since he asked it as they were walking companionably to her door, Skid trailing behind them at the end of his leash.

"I never said you were irresponsible." Thought it, yes, Sabrina told herself. But she'd never say it out loud. Not to Tommy's face.

"Yes, you did. Last night when I brought you home."

"I don't remember saying that."

"I'm not surprised."

Sabrina waved a hand as if to brush her wayward words from Tommy's mind. "It was the allergy pill. It has that effect on some people. I called my doctor and he said to try taking only half from now on."

"Forget it."

"Tommy, I didn't mean to hurt you. It's just that. . . ." Sabrina sighed. How could she ever explain herself?

"You said I was too much fun, too," Tommy reminded her.

Sabrina was feeling worse by the minute. "Did I say anything nice? Anything?"

Tommy gave her that slow smile that melted her bones. "As a matter of fact, you did. You said I was a nice guy. And that I smell good."

He took a step closer. Sabrina got a whiff of Tommy's special blend of animal, fresh air, and man.

"So, see there. Honesty can be a good thing." Sabrina's nerves were shot by the time he slid his arms around her waist.

Tommy bent his head. Oh, dear. Oh, no. He was going to kiss her. Again. She needed one of those robots like the one on *Lost in Space* to wave its arms and shout, "Warning! Warning! Danger, Will Robinson." Only in her case it would shout "Danger, Sabrina Talbott!"

Even as that alarm inside her went off, she tilted her head up for his kiss. It didn't matter that he wasn't the guy for her. That he was an irresponsible party animal. That he so clearly wasn't her type.

His lips touched hers and she melted against him. Her arms slid around his shoulders.

"Woof!"

Sabrina became vaguely aware of something wiggling against her legs, separating her from Tommy's embrace.

She opened her eyes and Tommy released her. It was all she could do not to moan her disappointment when he let go.

"He's got lousy timing, doesn't he?" Tommy indicated the dog who now sat between them, wagging his tail. He lifted a paw to Tommy's jeans-clad leg as if in apology.

"Rotten mutt," Sabrina whispered under her breath. Skid was probably trying to pay her back for encouraging Tommy to enroll him in obedience classes.

It was just as well, she told herself. She had no future with Tommy Cameron. Any further involvement would just lead to heartbreak. And she'd still have to live next door to him.

"I'm really not as irresponsible as you think I am."

"Tommy, whatever I said, I never meant to imply—"

"I know Skid dug up your flowers. And your black eye is my fault. And if I hadn't been tickling you, you wouldn't have a split lip. But I promised to make it up to you. Let me cook you dinner. How about tomorrow night?"

"That's really not necessary. You don't have to prove anything to me."

"Maybe not. But come and have dinner with me anyway."

Sabrina waffled. Dinner at Tommy's house was too much like a date. "I don't think so."

"Are you going to make me beg? Because if you are, I'm warning you, I'm very good at it. I learned from the master. Didn't I, Skid?"

Skid gave him a sharp bark in reply. Which almost sounded like an affirmative response to Sabrina.

"Tom—uh, Tommy, don't take this the wrong way. I think dating you is a bad idea."

"Why? Because I'm a bad influence? Besides, who said anything about dating?" Tommy's eyes sparkled with feigned innocence.

I did, Sabrina thought. "No one."

"Fine. Now, will you come to dinner tomorrow?"

Tommy gave in much too easily. A wave of disappointment swept through Sabrina. If he had no romantic interest

in her, then why had he kissed her? Not once, but twice
during their brief acquaintance. But what had she expected?
Tommy lived in the moment. He wouldn't give a thought
to their future separately or together. Romantically or otherwise. Easy come, easy go. If one woman turned him
down, he'd just look around for another. He probably did
it all the time. She gasped as she remembered something
he'd mentioned to her the day they'd met. Something she'd
conveniently forgotten until now.

"Wait a minute. What about your fiancée?"

"My *what?*"

"Fiancée. If you're engaged to be married, why are you
inviting me to dinner?" *And why did you kiss me? And take
me out for dinner and dog obedience classes and ice
cream?* Two-timing Tommy. That's who he was.

"Who told you I was engaged?"

"You did. The day we met."

Tommy's brow furrowed and then cleared. "No. What I
said was I planned to have a wife pretty soon."

"So what does that mean? You're engaged to be engaged?"

Tommy chuckled. "I'm not engaged. Or engaged to be
engaged. Marriage is part of my five-year plan. That's all."

"*You* have a five-year plan?"

"Sure. You can't just drift through life. At some point
you have to be an adult. You have to think about the future."

Sabrina tried to hide her shock. Who'd have thought
Tommy Cameron had a five-year plan? She wasn't sure he
even had a job. She wasn't sure she could handle friendship
with a man like him. But in the interest of good neighborhood relations, she had to try, didn't she?

*   *   *

When she knocked on Tommy's screen door the following evening, he called for her to come in.

Skid rushed to greet her and she paused to rub him behind the ears. He gave her his goofy grin, tongue lolling out of his mouth.

Skid led the way through the house to the kitchen and then to the small back room where Tommy and his friends had been setting up computer equipment and shelves the night of the party.

Sabrina gazed around at the space which now looked like a well-organized office. Shelving units lined the walls amidst file cabinets and other business paraphernalia.

Tommy's back was to her, and over his shoulder she could see he was playing a computer game. Spaceships flew across the screen while he worked the controls, trying to eliminate them with red laser beams.

"I'll just be a minute," he said, his eyes never leaving the screen.

It figures, Sabrina thought. Didn't he have anything better to do with his time than play computer games? How did the man make a living?

And if the absence of dinner preparation in his kitchen was any indication, she had a feeling they'd be dining on delivered pizza again.

Tommy Cameron's idea of responsibility and hers were two entirely separate things. He had to be conning her with that five-year-plan story.

"Ah ha! Gotcha!" Tommy addressed this comment to the computer screen. Had he succeeded in blowing up all the spaceships in record time? Sabrina wondered. He'd probably turn around and give her a high five now.

But he didn't. Instead he made a few notes on a pad near his elbow. His fingers then flew across the keyboard. The video game disappeared, replaced with lines of letters and symbols.

Sabrina could not make heads or tails of the scrolling screen, but Tommy apparently knew what he was doing. After about five minutes, he closed the screen and turned to greet her.

"Sorry about that."

"Oh, that's okay. It's about what I expected."

She followed him into the kitchen. He withdrew a bottle of ginger ale from the refrigerator and opened it.

"What's about what you expected?"

"That you'd be playing computer games. And that you probably forgot you invited me to dinner. What are we having anyway? Pizza from Luigi's again? Or is Chung Woo's delivering moo goo gai pan later?"

"You think you've got it all figured out, don't you, Sabrina?"

Tommy poured ginger ale into two glasses and handed her one. His tone was light, but she knew she'd annoyed him.

She took an uncertain sip of her soft drink.

"You were playing a computer game when I arrived, weren't you?"

He fixed her with a look. Not the lazy, casual look, either. Or the one with the glittering heat. This one was more curious, more controlled.

"Yes, I was playing a computer game. That's what I do for a living. I design computer games. And I do consulting. I create software. That particular game is not one I designed. The manufacturer sent it to me after they discovered a flaw in it. I found the problem just as you arrived."

"Oh."

Tommy gave her a measuring look, his brows knit together in irritation.

"And for your information." He turned back to the refrigerator and withdrew a bowl filled with an elaborate salad. Next to that he placed a platter where two thick steaks were marinating. He held up two baking potatoes for her inspection. Then a loaf of bakery bread. Next came a plate of sliced mushrooms and onions. "For the steaks," he said.

"So we're not having pizza?" Sabrina's voice squeaked just the tiniest bit, the way it always did when she knew she owed someone an apology.

"No. We're not having pizza."

How could she have been so wrong? She'd made a snap judgment about Tommy the moment she'd met him and followed through on it ever since. Evidently, there was more to Tommy Cameron than met the eye. *Her* eye, at least.

"So what have you got to say for yourself, Miss Smarty Pants?"

"I'm sorry?"

"What was that? I couldn't hear you."

"I said I'm sorry. I jumped to conclusions. It won't happen again."

He frowned as if he didn't quite believe her, then excused himself for a moment. Before he reappeared, soft jazz filled the rooms of his house. It wasn't classical music, nor the slow kind of dance tunes she recalled from the night of the party, but sort of a combination of both.

"None of Metallica's greatest hits this evening?" she asked when he returned to the kitchen.

"Goober's the Metallica fan, not me."

He dumped the onions and mushrooms into a skillet and

set it on a burner on low heat. Then he set the potatoes in the microwave oven and punched a couple of buttons.

"Goober?"

"Eugene Davies. I guess you don't remember him from the other day."

"No, I guess not. Why do you call him Goober?"

"I honestly can't remember how he got that nickname. But knowing Goober, there's probably a good reason."

"You don't sound like you have a very high opinion of him," Sabrina commented as she followed Tommy outside. A grill was already hot with coals piled in the center. He poked and prodded them until they were arranged to his satisfaction. The steaks sizzled as he laid them across the rack.

"I've known all those guys since elementary school. Goober's part of that crowd. I'll be the first to admit he's not perfect, but then, who is? He's got his good points. It just takes me a while to remember what they are."

Tommy turned back to the steaks and Sabrina got the hint. He didn't want to talk about his friends anymore. Everything she'd said so far this evening had come out as an insult, and she knew without a doubt her best move would be to shut up.

The oven timer beeped at about the same time he finished grilling the steaks. The mushrooms and onions had cooked nicely with a minimum of attention. Sabrina sipped her second glass of ginger ale.

She hadn't lifted a finger because Tommy had everything organized. The table on his screened back porch was set for two, with napkins and utensils, and candles, even. Amazing.

Sabrina tried to remember the last time a man had cooked for her and couldn't. She was pretty sure that was because it had never happened before. It was a pleasant experience, however. One she wouldn't mind repeating.

In fact, no one ever cooked for her. She ate alone most of the time. If she dined with friends, they went out to restaurants.

She didn't feel compelled to make idle chitchat during dinner, which would have been impossible, with her mouth full most of the time. Besides, she didn't want to take a chance on saying the wrong thing again.

When she finished she sat back, relaxed and satiated. It was almost dark. The candles glowed in the middle of the table. "This was very pleasant. Thank you. I hate to eat and run, but I have an early day tomorrow."

"No problem. I'll walk you home."

"That's really not necessary."

"I know. But it's the friendly, neighborly thing to do."

When they reached her porch, she turned to Tommy. "Thank you for dinner. It was wonderful. Really. And I'm—I'm really sorry, I always seem to say the wrong things to you."

She supposed he wouldn't try to kiss her good night. Maybe he'd offer her a cold, clinical handshake. She winced internally. She'd rather have the kiss.

"I won't even try to kiss you good night," Tommy said.

What was this? Was he reading her mind?

"Since we're just going to be friends. And neighbors."

"Friends and neighbors. Right." What was worse? Monosyllabic but original responses? Or repeating everything Tommy said?

"I could give you a hug, though, couldn't I? That would be pretty friendly. And neighborly. Wouldn't it?"

He was gazing at her with a combination of warmth and intensity.

"A hug. Sure." Monosyllabic *and* repetitive. Definitely the way to go.

Tommy stepped closer. He wrapped his arms around her. Sabrina slid her arms around his waist and pressed her cheek to his chest. She could get used to the soft cotton of all his well-worn T-shirts. Could get used to his arms around her; to being held just like this.

Warning, Sabrina Talbott. *Danger! Danger!* The voice of her internal alarm went off again. But what had her security system done for her, anyway? She'd been listening to those internal warnings for years and look where she was. Alone. Eating crumpets and drinking tea by herself. Waiting for Mr. Perfect.

"I know I'm not supposed to. But I'd really like to kiss you."

"You would?" Sabrina's response was muffled against his chest, but she started to tingle all over at just the thought of Tommy kissing her again.

"Yeah, I would. I like kissing you."

"You do?" She managed to pry her head away from his chest and look up at him.

"Yeah. I do."

He started slow, like he was afraid she was going to tell him no. Yeah, right, thought Sabrina. Like she really hated the way his kisses made her feel. Tingly and warm and melty all at the same time.

Tommy cradled her head in his hands, his fingers in her hair. His lips touched hers and her mind drifted off to somewhere warm, safe, and secure. Tommy's tenderness made her feel cherished and special. The kiss ended much too soon.

He drew back slowly, combing his fingers through her

hair. Reluctantly, Sabrina opened her eyes. She could barely function. Her knees were wobbly.

Tommy said, "Well, good night. Neighbor."

Sabrina nodded. She was sure she did. She could feel her head moving up and down. But not even a monosyllabic response escaped her this time.

Once Sabrina closed her door, Tommy sauntered back to his house, thumbs tucked into the pockets of his jeans.

When had it become Priority One to prove to Sabrina that she was wrong about him? Why did he care so much what she thought of him? It shouldn't matter if she thought he was irresponsible. But it did. He certainly enjoyed proving her wrong.

Did she really think he did nothing but sit around and play computer games all day? Well, he admitted to himself, he sort of did. But not for entertainment. At least not exclusively. His design and consulting business was going like gangbusters. He liked the freedom of setting his own hours and working out of his home. The money was good and his clients were reliable.

That didn't make him irresponsible, did it? Just because he didn't put on a shirt and a tie every day and commute to a job he hated so he could work himself into an early grave.

No. Sabrina just had some weird ideas about the kind of man she ought to be dating. She'd convinced herself he wasn't her type for some reason.

Hmmpf! He opened the door to his house. Skid's nails tap-tapped as he followed him back to the kitchen, where Tommy started to clean up. Not her type, my eye.

She sure doesn't kiss me like I'm not her type. And she sure didn't object to spending the evening with me or letting me cook dinner for her.

Indeed, she'd been like a delighted child when she saw the effort he'd gone to. She'd eaten every bite and raved about the meal. Tommy had thoroughly enjoyed pampering her. Maybe he'd do it again soon. Very soon.

Maybe he'd come up with a few more surprises for his new neighbor. He'd seen the appraising glances she'd given the interior of his house. Compared with her polished antiques, his beat-up bachelor pad furniture must look truly pathetic. And he'd yet to see her wear a pair of jeans. No, her clothes were all spic and span, neatly pressed in matching colors. Sabrina was the conventional type. A place for everything and everything in its place.

He could just imagine the kind of guys Sabrina usually dated. Stuffy, boring types, never a hair out of place or a scuff on a shoe. The kind of guys who figured out a twenty-percent tip to the penny and drove sensible sedans.

No wonder she thought he wasn't her type. No wonder she thought him irresponsible. Comfort came first with him and his friends. And following at a close second was enjoying life.

She wasn't impressed with his friends, either, although she hadn't seen them at their best. And she didn't think much of Skid, but then Skid hadn't been terribly well behaved in her presence. On the other hand, he couldn't imagine that fluffy cat of hers lifting a paw to dig up a neighbor's rosebush. Skid should at least get some points for his enthusiasm.

Well, whatever Sabrina thought of him, he had a pretty good idea how he could change her mind. And if he did it well, she wouldn't suspect a thing.

He envisioned what was left of his five-year plan. Sabrina would fit into it quite nicely, he thought. Once he finished training her.

Chapter Ten

A*ny dog can be trained.* That's what the instructor assured the participants of the class Tuesday night. Praise and reward were the most effective means of changing a dog's behavior. The owner should use consistent but gentle discipline when needed.

The trainer had reiterated to the dog owners that the road to a well-behaved pet was simply a matter of patience, consistency, and persistence. Even the most unruly animal, with the proper amount of discipline and praise, could become the pet of one's dreams. But what if the animal were human? And male?

"What's with you?"

Sabrina glanced up as Elaine halted in her office doorway.

Sabrina had been gazing out the window of her office, tapping the eraser end of a pencil against her lips, daydreaming. Wondering if Tommy Cameron could be trained. If somehow she could turn him into Mr. Perfect. What a completely ludicrous idea.

She summoned herself back to reality.

"Nothing's with me. I was just thinking, that's all."

Elaine leaned against the doorjamb, tilted her blond head to one side in interest, and crossed her arms over her chest. "About what?"

"About my new neighbor, if you must know." Sabrina gave her a rueful look.

"Your new guy neighbor? The good-looking one with the dog? Do tell." Elaine scooted from the doorway to the chair next to Sabrina's desk and settled herself in anticipation.

"There's nothing to tell, really."

"Ha!" Elaine scoffed. "You're staring off into space in the middle of the day and you're thinking about him. Come on, Sabrina. Don't hold out on me."

Sabrina smiled. Since Elaine's break-up six months ago with the most recent in a long line of unsuitable boyfriends, she'd been living vicariously through her friends' relationships.

"He's nice, right?"

"Yes, Elaine. He's very nice."

"And good looking."

"Good looking. Yes."

"And single."

"Yes, Elaine. He's single. As far as I know."

"As far as you know?" Elaine was ultrasensitive on this particular issue, having been duped more than once by two-timing men.

Sabrina shrugged. "There doesn't seem to be a permanent female fixture in his life at the moment."

"And you're wondering why not?"

Sabrina squirmed and decided to be completely honest. "He could probably have ten women hanging on him if he wanted."

"Maybe he doesn't want."

"Yes. Maybe." Sabrina nibbled the inside of her bottom lip.

"So? What's the problem?"

"The problem is I told him I didn't want to date him. That I just wanted to be friends."

"Why, for heaven's sake? He sounds perfect!"

Sabrina squirmed some more. "You know about the party."

Elaine fluttered her hand through the air as if to say, yes, that was old news. "So he had a party. And the music was too loud. He turned it down, didn't he?"

"Yes. But then there's his dog—"

"Who dug up your roses. He replaced them, didn't he?"

"Yes."

"What else?"

"He kissed me," Sabrina confessed.

"And you're complaining?" Elaine raised her eyebrows. "Oh, I get it. He's a lousy kisser?"

"No."

"He's a good kisser?"

Sabrina nodded miserably.

"Then what's the problem?"

"I don't know." Anxiety gripped Sabrina. She'd thought talking to Elaine would make her feel better. Instead, it was making her feel worse, forcing her to question exactly why getting any closer to Tommy Cameron terrified her. She fell back on her standard excuse. "He's really not my type."

"Why? Afraid he might shake up your perfect little world?" Elaine gave her a piercing look.

"What's that supposed to mean?"

"Exactly what I said. You've created your own insulated world. Let's call it Sabrinaland. Where everything is just so. Exactly the way Sabrina wants it. There's just one problem. Sabrina's in there alone. She doesn't let anyone else in."

"Elaine! That's not true!"

Elaine tilted her head. "Really? When's the last time you had a serious relationship with a man?"

"I date." Sabrina sat back in her chair, refusing to dignify Elaine's question with any further response. Or the truth.

"Ha! You date. But you never get seriously involved. When's the last time you invited a guy into your house?"

"Saturday."

"Saturday? Who was it? The Maytag repairman?"

Sabrina thrust her bottom lip forward. "Tommy."

"Your neighbor?" Elaine started to giggle.

"What are you laughing at?"

Elaine shook her head. "Nothing. I swear." She was grinning from ear to ear. She had a knowing gleam in her eye that vaguely reminded Sabrina of some of Tommy's expressions. As if Elaine too were testing her and she'd somehow passed. Elaine leaned forward and covered Sabrina's hand with one of her own, an urgent tone in her voice. "You know how you're always joking about finding your very own Mr. Perfect?"

Sabrina nodded. To her it wasn't a joke.

"What if you're so busy searching for Mr. Perfect that Mr. Almost Perfect slips right by you?"

"Elaine, if you're trying to tell me Tommy is Mr. Almost

Perfect, forget it. He's a nice guy, but he's really, *really* not my type."

"Okay, then. If you're sure. But does Tommy have any friends? Single guy friends?"

Sabrina could only too clearly recall the pack of men at his party and playing football on his front lawn.

"I'm sure he does. In fact, I think he has quite a few."

Elaine sat forward. "Really? Are any of them like your Tommy? Could you set me up with one of them?"

"Elaine, I don't really know Tommy's friends, but I don't think anyone in his crowd would be your type." Sabrina thought of the guy nicknamed Goober and shuddered. Definitely not him. "And he's not 'my Tommy.' "

"Sabrina, come on. Share the wealth. I'm desperate, here. Would you ask him? For me?"

Elaine was a good person. A smart woman. One date with any of Tommy's unsuitable friends and surely she'd see, just as Sabrina had with Tommy, that they weren't right for her.

"I can ask him. For you. I wouldn't do it for just anybody, you know," Sabrina groused jokingly.

Elaine jumped up and gave her a quick hug. "Oh, thank you, thank you, thank you, Sabrina. I have a good feeling about this."

I don't, Sabrina thought gloomily as Elaine fairly skipped from her office and back down the hallway. She just hoped Elaine had learned by now how to guard her heart.

Sabrina tried not to be disappointed when she didn't see Tommy that evening. She told herself she wouldn't go out of her way to look for him.

Her rosebushes were all still standing. She should be glad, shouldn't she? Then why did she experience such a let-down as she paused to check them over before she went inside?

She brewed tea, put *The Best of Beethoven* on the stereo, but she couldn't relax. The music irritated her, and the tea tasted sour.

Victoria, as if sensing her mood, meowed constantly in inquiry. The cat was getting on her nerves even more than usual.

Sabrina poured the tea down the drain and scraped the remainder of her crumpet into the garbage. She snapped the stereo off and dug through her CDs and tapes for something that wouldn't annoy her.

Not finding anything to her taste, she turned on the radio and skimmed the channels until she found some soft rock. *Slow dance music?* her subconscious seemed to inquire. *You never listen to that station.* Oh, shut up, she told it.

She wished she had a non-diet soda. And maybe some potato chips.

What's *wrong* with me, she wondered. She never ate potato chips. She prided herself on her disciplined schedule. Regular exercise. Nutritious meals. At least she'd been disciplined before she met Tommy.

Pizza. Ice cream. Steak and potatoes. He was wreaking havoc with her carefully cultivated self-control.

She was sure the blame for this current craving she had for potato chips could be laid directly at his door. Tommy Cameron was a bad influence. Everyone knew potato chips were loaded with fat and salt. And the amount of sugar in regular soda was truly abominable.

But that's what we want, her taste buds insisted.

Ignoring her cravings, Sabrina took her bulging briefcase upstairs and unloaded the stack of essays she needed to wade through and grade.

Potato chips and soda would make the task a lot more pleasurable.

Sabrina's feet led her back downstairs to her purse and her keys, and finally to her car.

Forty-five minutes later, she returned. Reviewing the cache of no-no purchases unloaded on the counter, she wanted to be truly appalled with herself. But she couldn't quite manage it.

A bag of potato chips. A two-liter bottle of regular soda. A chocolate bar. Frozen pizza. She didn't even want to know the fat content of that. And a box of cellophane-wrapped cakes. Less than a week in Tommy Cameron's company and she'd become a junk-food junkie.

Why did I buy these little cakes, she wondered as she unwrapped one. *Why am I eating one?* She sank her teeth into the soft sponge cake filled with cream and leaned back against the refrigerator.

"Oh, wow." She took another bite. "Yum." She finished it off and licked her fingers. "Okay, we'll just tuck these babies away for later," she told Victoria, who sat watching her through slitted eyes as she buried the box of mini sponge cakes in the back of the cupboard.

"Now then." She poured an ice-filled glass full of soda and took the bag of potato chips upstairs with her. "We're off to work."

As she got into bed that night, Sabrina felt so satisfied after her junk-food binge she easily ignored the twinge of guilt she felt for pigging out. "It was only this one time. It won't happen again."

She turned out the light and settled down in bed.

She could hear television noise coming through her window from Tommy's house next door. She knew the layout of the McDermotts' house. The master bedroom was right across from hers. And these old houses had been built when big windows were the fashion.

She rolled over and separated the blinds covering her window to peek out.

Tommy's lights were on. His bedroom curtains were open. The television flickered light and shadows around the room. The murmur of dialogue sounded like commentary on a baseball game.

Tommy wandered in, toothbrush in mouth. He wore a pair of drawstring pajama bottoms and nothing else. Sabrina's mouth fell open as she got her first glimpse of exactly what lay beneath those T-shirts he always wore. Tommy worked out. She'd bet her life on it. She stared at the well-defined muscles of his chest, shoulders, and arms. Washboard abs. Her mouth went dry.

A commercial came on and Tommy wandered back into the bathroom. Disgusted with herself, Sabrina closed her blinds, reached for the glass of water on her nightstand, and drank half of it. She'd never been so affected by a man before. So why was she so fascinated by a man who was so obviously wrong for her? *Because he's a hunk,* a little voice inside her head answered.

This had to stop.

She stared up at the ceiling, silently requesting forgiveness for spying on her neighbor. She promised herself she wouldn't do it again. She'd tell Tommy the lights from his bedroom window kept her awake and would he please close his curtains from now on.

Of course she would.

First chance she got.

Chapter Eleven

The following morning Sabrina dressed with her usual care. Since she had no first-period class, she had decided to pay Tommy a visit on Elaine's behalf. She knew Elaine would pester her until she set her up with one of Tommy's buddies.

She ignored that little voice that told her she was glad of the excuse—any excuse—to see Tommy. But her heart sped up anyway when she knocked on Tommy's door. Perhaps he was still in bed. Tough. He should be up at a respectable hour like everyone else, ready to put in a full-day's work. Unbidden came the memory of Tommy's sleepy brown eyes when he'd answered the door the other day, a cup of coffee in his hand. Maybe he liked to work at night and sleep all day.

She glanced around and noticed Tommy's porch needed to be painted. The summer sun picked up every nick and crack in the weathered finish. After his surgery, Mr. McDermott hadn't been able to keep the house up the way he used to.

Tommy should put a trellis on the east end of the porch, she mused. Plant some climbing roses there next spring so they'd catch the morning sun. He had plenty of room for a porch swing too. Maybe a couple of wicker chairs.

The door opened. A woman in a bathrobe appeared, her hair wrapped in a towel.

Sabrina stared at the woman's rounded abdomen.

"May I help you?" the stranger asked.

Remembering her manners, she caught herself and brought her gaze back to the woman's face. "I, uh, is Tommy here?"

"No. He ran out for donuts. He should be back any minute. Whom shall I say . . . ?"

"Oh. Um. Would you tell him Sabrina from next door—"

"Sabrina!" The woman opened the screen door. "I should have known. You're perfect. Just the way Tommy described you. Come on in."

Sabrina followed the woman inside, listening as she chattered all the way to the kitchen. "How about some coffee? Sorry. It's decaf." She held up the pot with one hand and patted her round tummy with the other. "Kids can't take the real thing, so they tell me."

She poured Sabrina a mug. "Cream? Sugar?"

"No. This is fine." Not knowing what else to do, Sabrina took a sip.

"I'm sorry. I should introduce myself. I'm Pam Kalinsky." Pam stuck out her hand and Sabrina shook it.

"Sabrina Talbott."

Pam grinned. "Yes. I know. Tommy's hardly talked about anything or anyone else since I got here last night."

Sabrina didn't know what to say. Why would Tommy be telling this Pam person anything about her? She took another sip of her coffee. Pam tilted her head to one side, in the same way Elaine had the other day. Sabrina told herself not to squirm.

"I'm sorry. I'm being rude. Come sit." She indicated the table. "You really are too perfect."

"I doubt that." Sabrina was getting tired of people telling her she was perfect. Hard as she tried, she knew better than anyone that she was not.

"Probably not," Pam agreed easily. "But you look that way. I love the sailor suit, by the way. And the anchor earrings. And look at this." She lifted Sabrina's wrist. "Even a nautical bracelet. Sailboats. Everything matches."

Sabrina squirmed. The outfit was one of her favorites. A navy blue rayon-blend suit, with a blue-and-white-striped tank top. The gold trim and buttons didn't exactly make it a "sailor suit," but she thought the accessories comple-mented it. The bracelet was a souvenir her mother had sent after a recent Caribbean cruise. Was this Pam person going to pat her on the head, now, she wondered, since she looked so perfectly matched?

"So Tommy tells me you teach high school?" Pam rested her chin in her hand, her brown eyes alive with interest.

"Yes," Sabrina responded stiffly. "English literature." Who was this woman, anyway? And why was she in Tommy's house? In a bathrobe? So early in the morning? And *whose* child was she carrying?

"Do you enjoy it?"

"Yes. Of course." Sabrina was starting to feel like a bug being picked apart. At a decided disadvantage from an un-known predator.

"I hear you've had a couple of run-ins with Skid." Pam grinned.

"Yes. He seems to like . . . flowers."

Pam shook her head. "That poor mutt. Ever since Tommy rescued him, they've been inseparable."

"Rescued him?" Sabrina echoed.

"Didn't Tommy tell you? He found Skid about a year ago. He'd been hit by a car and left for dead. Tommy carted him off to the animal hospital. Poor dog had a broken leg, and I don't know what else. Internal injuries, probably. All I know is Tommy ended up with a huge vet bill. And ever since, he's spoiled the dog rotten.

"That's why he named him Skid. Skidmark. Ironic, huh?"

Pam chattered on. "I guess I can understand, sort of. It's like if you had a kid that was really sick, and you were afraid he was going to die. If he recovers, you want to give him everything, you're so happy he survived." She leaned forward. "Personally, though, I think that dog could use some discipline."

The subject of their conversation bounded in at that moment, wiggling in excitement at his two women guests. Pam ruffled the fur on his head and rubbed him under the chin. He swiped his tongue across her face before turning his attention to Sabrina. She rubbed his ears lightly, and pushed him back when he tried to bury his nose between her knees. He shook himself and a flurry of dog hair floated around his immediate vicinity, most of it landing on the navy blue of her suit.

She was brushing ineffectually at it when Tommy appeared, donut box in hand.

She looked up in time to see his expression change from one of surprise to . . . was that pleasure? She glanced from him to Pam in uncertainty. Tommy hadn't shaved yet, and the dark stubble paired with his unruly hair and T-shirt-and-jeans uniform reminded Sabrina of a modern day James Dean. Tommy had more than his usual air of mystery and mischief in his demeanor this morning. Sabrina didn't want to be intrigued and curious, but she was.

"Howdy, neighbor." He set the box of donuts on the table.

"Good morning, Tommy." She knew she sounded stiff and formal, but she wasn't at all comfortable with this pregnant woman in Tommy's house. Pam acted quite at home in Tommy's kitchen, and there was an ease between them of long acquaintance.

Tommy and Pam exchanged looks and smiles. And if Sabrina wasn't mistaken, there was a slight roll of the eyes on both their parts.

Tommy moved to pour himself coffee. "This is a pleasant surprise. Finding you here."

Sabrina wasn't sure which of them he meant. "Me? Or Pam?"

Tommy and Pam chuckled. Sabrina's gaze swung between the two of them, trying to puzzle out the shared joke.

Tommy took a seat at the table and opened the donut box. "You. I already knew Pam was here. She got in last night."

"Oh." There was a connection of some sort between the two of them Sabrina knew she wasn't getting.

"Have you two known each other long?" she asked. Tommy pushed the donut box in her direction, but she shook her head. After last night's feast, no way could she eat a donut.

Pam, however, had no such reserve. She picked up a chocolate-covered one and bit into it.

"All our lives." Tommy smiled fondly at Pam. "Didn't Pam tell you?"

Pam nodded, her mouth full, returning an affectionate gaze of her own.

"Childhood sweethearts? Is that it?"

Pam choked on her donut and covered her mouth with her hand. Tommy's coffee mug stopped midair, his brows knit in confusion for a second before a grin split his face.

Pam managed to swallow and started to giggle. Tommy chuckled. Sabrina couldn't imagine what was so funny, and neither of them rushed to explain it to her. She felt a blush spread up her cheeks. She was embarrassed, but she didn't know why. All she wanted to do was escape the two of them and their private joke. She was pretty sure it was at her expense.

She pushed her chair back and stood. "If you'll excuse me." She didn't look at either of them directly. She couldn't. The feeling of mortification went too deep.

By the time she reached the front door, tears were threatening. Of course, Tommy would have a girlfriend. A relationship. He wasn't wearing a ring, but for all she knew he might even be married. He claimed he wasn't engaged to be engaged, but obviously it wasn't true. The two-timing, no-good, immature, irresponsible—

"Hey, Bree, wait up. Where are you going?"

She could hear Tommy calling to her as the screen slammed behind her. Skid's nails skittered across the wood as he bounded out of the house with his master. What she wanted at the moment was to be as far away from him—them—as possible. Forever. She'd sell her house. She'd move. Just so she'd never have to see Tommy Cameron or his dog again.

"Sabrina!"

She'd barely reached the divide between their properties before he caught up with her.

He grasped her elbow and she jerked away from him.

"Any female in heat, huh, Tommy? That's about what I figured. How many other girlfriends do you have?"

"What girlfriends?"

"How many other children on the way? How many are already here? Or do you even know? Do you even take responsibility for them after they arrive?"

"What? Wait. Bree. Slow down."

"Don't call me 'Bree!' I'm not one of your girls. I'm Sabrina to you. Or Ms. Talbott."

Sabrina had herself so worked up, she couldn't think straight. Just the idea of another woman in Tommy's arms made her sick. He was more irresponsible than she'd originally thought. Didn't he realize how many other people were affected by his behavior? Didn't he care?

"Whoa. Whoa. Slow down there, Miss Smarty Pants. I don't have any kids. And I don't have any girlfriends. Because the one woman I'm interested in won't go out with me. She thinks I'm immature and irresponsible. And, oh yes. That I'm not her type."

Tommy's eyes blazed down at her as they faced each other in the morning light.

Sabrina's mouth moved, but she couldn't get words to come out. Not even monosyllabic ones. Finally, a couple shook themselves loose from her tongue. "But—but—what about—Pam?"

"My sister. My visiting from Chicago, baby due in three weeks, older sister. She drove down last night."

"But I thought—"

"I know what you thought." Tommy's expression was grim.

"Well, how was I supposed to know?" Sabrina cried, her outrage refreshed, recalling how humiliated she'd felt—like the "other woman"—caught between their cozy familiarity.

"You weren't, I suppose. I just assumed Pam told you we were related."

"Well, she didn't! I thought—you let me believe that you and she—oh!" Sabrina pressed the palms of her hands to her flaming cheeks. Tears threatened. Tears of relief. Or maybe exasperation.

She turned away. "Just forget it." She refused to cry on Tommy's shoulder again. On her front lawn. For all the world to see.

She took two steps. Three. "Bree."

He was right there next to her.

"Go away."

"I'm sorry." He draped an arm over her shoulder and walked with her. Sabrina dashed at the tears with her fingertips. What was wrong with her anyway? She never lost control like this. And for the second time in less than a week, Tommy Cameron was the reason.

He followed her up the steps, then turned to look at her.

Gently he swiped at the mascara smeared under her eyes. "Messed you up again, didn't I?" he asked softly. Tommy smiled as he trailed his thumbs along her cheeks before he let go of her and tapped an index finger under her chin. "So what brought you by this morning?"

"Oh. Um. Nothing. It wasn't important."

"You're blushing. Must have been something."

Sabrina sighed and crossed her arms over her chest. "My friend Elaine. She wanted me to ask if you had any single friends she could meet."

"Ah. And you told her I had lots of them. And that they're all just as irresponsible as I am, right?"

Sabrina winced. Tommy's assessment came too close to the truth. "I told her I'd ask you."

"I take that as a positive sign."

"Why?"

"Because it means you've been talking to your friend about me."

"So?" Sabrina challenged. "You've been talking to your sister about me. You told her I was perfect."

Tommy grinned. "So I did. I also told her how much I enjoy messing you up every once in awhile." He lightly tousled the hair on top of her head.

"Stop it." There was no force or annoyance behind her words. She bit her lip to keep from smiling.

"As a matter of fact, I'm having a party Friday night."

"*Another one?*"

"For Pam. She wants to see all the old gang."

"Oh."

"Tell your friend Elaine she's invited. She can have her pick of my single buddies. Frankie Long's probably her best bet."

"Okay. I'll tell her. Thank you."

"And Sabrina?"

"Yes?"

"You'll come, won't you?"

"I wouldn't miss it for the world."

"You really ought to lighten up more often, Sabrina."

She chewed the inside of her lip. Her eyes slid away from him in annoyance. His words had pushed a button she'd almost forgotten was there.

"Well, that was definitely the wrong thing to say."

She regarded him coolly. "Yes. It was."

"I promise not to tell you to lighten up again. Will you still come to the party?"

"Yes."

"And you'll dance with me?"

Sabrina blushed again. "Yes."

"Good." Tommy bent over and brushed a kiss across her cheek. He stepped off the porch, then stopped. Skid lay on Sabrina's walk looking exceedingly pleased with himself.

Tommy turned back. "Sabrina?"

"Yes?"

"I think we'll need to make another trip to the garden center." He stooped, picked up a bedraggled plant from the lawn, and held it up for her to see. "This isn't a rosebush, is it?"

Sabrina shook her head. "No. It's a hydrangea."

Another piece of her garden destroyed. Why wasn't she more upset?

Chapter Twelve

"Can I move in with you, Sabrina?"

Sabrina finished fastening a hoop earring into her lobe and glanced over her shoulder. Elaine sat with one hip on the windowsill, gazing out at the house next door.

"Come away from the window, would you? You're fogging up the glass."

Elaine didn't budge from her perch. "The view is much too good. How can you stand it?"

For the past half hour Elaine had been watching the guests stream toward Tommy's house next door. "Which one is Frankie?"

"I don't know. The one who's the most on the ball, I expect, since Tommy recommended him."

"Is he anything like Tommy?"

"I don't know, Elaine. I barely met him." Sabrina vaguely recalled the glimpses she'd had of Tommy's guests

99

at the last party. He'd asked Frankie to change the music, but Sabrina had no memory of what Frankie Long looked like. And after the incident with the football, she'd been aware of only Tommy and her rapidly swelling black eye. Introductions to his friends had barely registered. "I'm sure he's darling," she assured Elaine.

"Can we go now?" Elaine's blond curls were almost bouncing in anticipation, like a little girl excited over a birthday party. She was probably looking forward to un-wrapping Frankie Long, Sabrina thought dryly. She didn't want Elaine to jump into anything, especially with an un-suitable guy. But she didn't know how she could prevent it. Elaine was a big girl.

"I'm ready. How do I look?"

"I hate you." Elaine sulked. "How come you always look so perfect?"

"I don't! Why does everyone keep saying that?" Sabrina knew for a fact that even though most of the bruising from her eye injury had faded, faint marks of yellowish purple remained beneath her makeup.

"Because you never have a hair out of place. It always does exactly what you want. Look how it curls under at the ends just so. And your clothes always match. Even your shoes. And you've got the perfect accessories for every outfit. And that flawless complexion. I hate you."

Sabrina gritted her teeth and took Elaine's arm, hustling her down the stairs. "Come on, let's go, before I get any more perfect."

Like a mother hen, Sabrina kept an eye on Elaine as she chatted with Frank Long, until Tommy called her on it.

He came up behind her and handed her a diet soda. "Frankie's a good guy. Stop worrying."

He looked over her shoulder to where Elaine and Frank

had their heads together across the room. They complemented each other. Frank had sandy blond hair and light blue eyes. His husky build seemed in tandem with Elaine's generous curves.

Sabrina turned to look at Tommy. "It's not Frank I'm worried about."

"Your friend Elaine doesn't need a guardian."

"How can you say that? You just met her."

"True. But I know you wouldn't be friends with someone irresponsible, untrustworthy, empty-headed, or uh, immature."

"That's right, I wouldn't," Sabrina snapped before she realized how neatly Tommy had trapped her into such an admission.

He grinned down at her. Sabrina wanted to be annoyed with him, but she was having too much fun.

It was true. Sabrina Talbott was having fun. At Tommy Cameron's party. For the second time in exactly a week. The difference was, the prospect no longer frightened her.

Tommy's friends were an easygoing crowd who accepted her appearance among them without question. Any friend of Tommy's is a friend of ours, their reception seemed to say.

Tommy's sister Pam had apologized profusely for their misunderstanding. Sabrina returned her sentiments, well aware of how quickly she'd made another of her incorrect snap judgments. She was more than happy to put the entire incident behind her.

This party wasn't as loud and boisterous as the one a week ago. The music was softer. People were talking instead of shouting. Pam was surrounded by several of the guests, engaged in animated conversation.

"Everyone has a good time at your parties, don't they?"

Sabrina asked, looking around at the assembled guests.

"Everyone but you," Tommy replied.

Sabrina turned back to him. "I'm having a good time," she protested. "Really."

Tommy shrugged. "If you say so. Look, Sabrina, I know this isn't your cup of tea." He grinned. "No pun intended."

"Oh, really? And just what is my 'cup of tea'?"

Tommy crossed his arms over his chest and leaned a shoulder against the wall, his brows knit in concentration as he appeared to give her question serious thought. "Your perfect evening? I'd guess dinner out. At a nice restaurant. One where they make the guys put on jackets if they aren't already wearing them. Where your date orders your meal, preferably in impeccable French."

Sabrina bit her lip.

"Everyone is quite dignified. If there's dancing, it's a waltz or a foxtrot to a small orchestra wearing white tuxedos. They don't sing," he added.

"Oh, come on, Tommy. I'm not that bad."

"And then," Tommy continued as if she hadn't interrupted, "your date drives you home in his sensible four-door sedan, walks you to the door. Kisses you." He waggled a finger in her face. "On the cheek, of course."

"Tommy!"

"Every day your dreamboat puts on a three-piece pin-striped suit, a button-down shirt, and a tie. While he's working from nine to five behind his desk at the bank or the law office or the CPA firm, he thinks about you. But, like a true gentlemen, he waits an appropriate number of days, three perhaps, before calling to ask you out again." He grinned. "How am I doing so far?"

Tommy had so perfectly pegged the guys she usually dated, especially the regular workday and the business suit,

Sabrina wondered if he'd had her investigated. But the way he described her idea of Mr. Perfect made him sound almost . . . boring! She pretended annoyance. "Really, Tommy. This isn't 1950!"

"No. You're right. And I'm not that guy." He lifted the glass of soda out of her hand and set it on a table. "Come on. They're playing our song."

Someone had dimmed the lights. And indeed the same slow dance tune as last week was playing once again. *They're playing our song.* Tommy's words reverberated through her head. Ridiculous, she assured herself. She and Tommy didn't have "a song." They didn't really have anything in common. Except undeniable attraction outweighed by definite unsuitability.

Tommy held her close. Sabrina's head swam and her knees grew weak. Tonight she refused to listen to her internal warning system. The only thing she was in danger of was falling madly in love with Tommy Cameron.

Maddening, somewhat irresponsible, perhaps a bit immature, freedom-loving, Tommy Cameron.

As the party wound down, Frank Long offered to drive Elaine home. Clever Elaine had insisted that Sabrina pick her up before the party, just in case she hit it off with Frank and wanted to prolong her time in his company.

Tommy walked Sabrina home as Pam bid good-bye to the last few guests lingering on the porch.

He made no move to embrace her, but instead offered her a handshake. "Thanks for coming to my party, neighbor."

The warmth of his hand engulfed hers. *This was it? No hug? No kiss? Not even on the cheek?*

"I enjoyed myself, Tommy. I really did."

Tommy didn't look convinced. He gave her a rueful

smile. "Maybe you were right, Sabrina. It might be awkward if we got . . . involved."

"Oh." Sabrina gulped back her disappointment.

"I'll see you around, okay?" Tommy stepped off the porch. "And I will replace your hydrangea. I won't forget."

Sabrina nodded miserably. "No rush."

She slid inside her door and collapsed against it. Who cared about a stupid hydrangea? She'd lost something much more important than one of her beloved flowers. She was very afraid she'd lost her heart to Mr. Not Perfect.

Victoria came up and rubbed against Sabrina's leg, fixing her with her blue eyes and meowing in a demand for acknowledgement.

Sabrina scooped the cat up before she could protest and buried her nose in Victoria's soft fur. Her heart was not going to be as easily replaced as her flowers.

Tommy followed Pam around the house holding a plastic garbage bag which she filled with empty cups and cans and used paper plates and napkins.

"It was good to see all the old gang again," Pam commented cheerfully. "Thanks for the party, Tommy."

"Yeah, sure. No problem."

Pam raised an eyebrow and glanced at her brother. "What's with you? You seem kind of down."

Tommy shrugged. "Nothing."

"Huh! You haven't been yourself since I arrived. Your new neighbor giving you a hard time?"

Tommy sighed as he followed Pam into the kitchen where they continued to work side by side cleaning up the party mess. "She says we should just be friends. Maybe she's right."

Pam picked up an empty pizza box and paused to glance up at Tommy. "Why 'just friends?' "

"Because she thinks if we got involved and it didn't work out it would be awkward since we're next-door neighbors."

"She's got a point, I suppose. But who says it wouldn't work out?" Pam filled the sink with soapy water.

"I don't know, Pammy. She's convinced I'm not her type."

Pam hooted with laughter and rolled her eyes. "She wouldn't think so if she could see your long face right now. Hasn't she noticed the way your eyes light up every time she walks in the room?" She glanced up at Tommy as he stood next to her, dish towel in hand. "Your lower lip's sticking out."

She rinsed a chip bowl and handed it to him, waiting for a reply.

"She thinks I'm irresponsible."

"What! Why?"

Tommy dried the bowl and set it on a cabinet shelf. "I don't know. She thinks all I want out of life is to have a good time."

Pam's eyebrow shot up again as she glanced Tommy's way. "Gee, I can't imagine why. Just because you've had parties two weekends in a row."

"One of which was because of you, don't forget," he said good-naturedly. "Sabrina doesn't really like parties."

"Oh, well, then, I can see why she doesn't think you're her type. But just for the record, she looked to me like she was enjoying herself tonight. Especially when the two of you were dancing."

"That's the thing. I'm getting all these mixed messages. She tells me she hates parties, but she told me she enjoyed herself tonight. She says I'm not her type, but when I kiss her—"

"Yes?"

"Never mind." Tommy turned to put another bowl away.

"Maybe Sabrina doesn't really know what she wants."

"She sure acts like she knows what she doesn't want. Me." He'd been thinking a lot lately about exactly what he wanted. He had wanted to kiss Sabrina earlier and regretted now that he hadn't. He wanted to believe she'd been disappointed that he didn't. But maybe she'd been relieved.

Pam chuckled. "Tommy, you grew up with three sisters and a mother. You should know by now that quite often we women don't know what we want until it lands in our lap. And then we decide it's *exactly* what we've been looking for all along."

He turned to her and smiled. "So are you saying when you give a woman what she thinks she wants, she doesn't want it anymore?"

"Exactly."

Tommy twisted a tie around the bulging garbage bag. Thanks to Pam a plan was emerging in his mind. "Sabrina thinks she wants a regular guy. You know, somebody conventional with a normal job. A suit-and-tie kind of guy with a sensible sedan."

Pam yawned.

"My thoughts exactly. She'll be bored to tears within six months if she ends up with a guy like that."

"So you think you can convince her what she really wants is a guy like you?"

"Not a guy *like* me," Tommy corrected. "*Me*."

"And you plan to do this how?"

"By becoming exactly what she thinks she wants. One of those conventional guys she claims are her type. By the time I'm finished, she'll be begging to have me back."

Pam smiled and nodded as she rinsed the last dish and let the water out of the sink.

"That's quite a plan, little brother. Too bad I won't be around to watch." She dried her hands. "I just hope you're not getting in over your head."

"Me too, Sis. Me too."

Chapter Thirteen

Sabrina lifted the lid on her mailbox and removed catalogs and envelopes. She shuffled through them absently before she went back inside.

"Howdy, neighbor."

Tommy came toward her, a shovel in one hand, a potted plant in the other.

Sabrina couldn't keep the smile off her face. Somehow the day seemed brighter when he was around. Her heart beat faster. She felt more alive. Did he have that affect on everyone, or was it just her?

She crossed the porch. "Hi, Tommy." She nodded toward the plant. "What's up?"

"This is a hydrangea, isn't it? They assured me that's what I was buying."

"Oh, yes, of course. It's a hydrangea."

Tommy tilted his head to the side and looked up at her,

his brow knit in puzzlement. "Don't you remember? Skid dug up one of yours the other day?"

"Uh-huh. Sure." In truth, she'd forgotten all about it. Could it be she'd become used to having her flowers dug up on a regular basis by the dog next door only to have her new neighbor replace them just as regularly?

"Right here okay?" Tommy indicated the approximate area vacated by the other hydrangea.

"Sure. That's fine." Sabrina sat on the top step and pretended to check her mail. She certainly wasn't going inside now. Not when she could spend some time with Tommy. From beneath her lashes she slid a glance his way. His hands curved around the handle of the shovel, his forearms flexed as he lifted a scoop of dirt.

She spotted a hand-addressed envelope she'd missed before and tore it open carefully.

She read the contents. "Oh, no! Not again."

Tommy glanced up. "What?"

Sabrina shook her head. "Nothing. It's just an invitation to a party."

Tommy lowered the hydrangea into the ground, patted the soil around it, and stood, brushing the dirt from his hands.

"Sabrina, we really have to talk. This problem you seem to have with parties, people having a good time, socializing—it's, well, it's just not normal."

"Trust me. If Principal Strickland's party is anything like last year, it won't be a good time."

"Principal?"

"Strickland. Every year he has a barbecue. A command performance. It's his way of keeping his thumb on the pulse of his staff."

"And you'd rather he not take your pulse?"

Sabrina shrugged. Last year, Bill Archer, the accountant she'd been dating at the time, refused to go with her. He abhorred barbecues, picnics, and pool parties. It didn't matter to Bill that Sabrina needed him as her escort. Had it been a soiree in a five-star restaurant his answer would have been a resounding yes. But Bill made it clear he had no intention of eating with his fingers, having a fly land in his drink, or being bitten by a mosquito. Bill wore perfectly tailored suits, he had a steady job, and drove a late-model sedan. He seemed stable and mature. Exactly what she was looking for. So what if he kept a lint brush in the glove compartment of his car, his desk drawer, and insisted one also be available for him at her house? So what if his idea of stimulating conversation was regaling her with a list of the latest tax-law changes? She needed a man who knew the importance of doing a job well, someone dedicated to earning a living so he could support a family someday.

She also needed someone who would be there for her when she needed him most. His refusal to attend the barbecue made it abundantly clear that Bill Archer was not that person. When she'd told him so, he'd politely asked her to return his lint brush and walked out the door.

Principal Strickland took a dateless Sabrina around with him on a mission to ask the other guests if they knew of any single men for her.

Her colleagues had been sympathetic after the fact, but Sabrina couldn't take the chance of it happening again.

"Sabrina? So what's the problem? Don't go."

"Oh, no. I have to go," she assured him. "I just need a—a—"

"A—a—what? A new outfit?"

Sabrina shook her head. "I need a date."

"Oh." Tommy sat on the step beside her and appeared

to contemplate her dilemma. "I'd help you out, Sabrina, but I know we can't date. I'm not your type. I'm too irresponsible and immature—"

"Tommy, stop it." She put her hand on his arm, feeling the warmth of his skin and the curly sprinkling of light hairs beneath her fingertips. "I'm never going to live that down, am I?" she asked. "Whatever I said that night, I apologize."

"And we live next door to each other."

"Meaning what?"

"According to you it means we can't date. Doesn't it?"

Sabrina chewed the inside of her lower lip. She tried to imagine what bringing Tommy Cameron into the midst of her staid, academic world would be like. Maybe, just maybe, if Tommy went to the Stricklands' party with her, it might be fun.

"Would you go with me?" she asked shyly, chancing a look at him from beneath her lashes.

"Aren't you afraid I'll embarrass you with my Neanderthal ways?"

"Tommy, stop it. You're not a Neanderthal. You're—you're—"

"The missing link?" Tommy joked.

Sabrina smiled. "Yeah." *You're my missing link.* She shied away from the thought. Tommy couldn't possibly be the piece of the puzzle she'd been missing in her life. He wasn't Mr. Perfect. He wasn't conventional and stable and fashionably dressed. He was carefree, spontaneous, and an expert in casual wear. But he was also Mr. Party Animal, which was exactly what she needed at the moment.

"When is this shindig?"

"This Saturday." Sabrina handed him the invitation. "Dress is casual, but—um. . . ." Her gaze swept his long legs covered in faded denim and his torso covered by yet another T-shirt, this one with the name of a local tractor dealer across the back.

"But not jeans and T-shirts," Tommy finished for her. "I get it, Sabrina." He chucked her gently under the chin. "Believe it or not, I can clean up my act when the occasion calls for it."

"I knew that," she lied.

"I'll think about it."

"You'll think about it?" Stunned, Sabrina stared at him. Didn't it just figure he'd be difficult when she most needed him to cooperate? "But you like parties," Sabrina reminded him. "You're good at them."

"Look, Sabrina, you've made it clear that you think I'm immature and irresponsible. You make fun of my name and my friends."

"I've never made fun of your friends!" Sabrina retorted hotly.

"Maybe not, but I know you don't think much of them. And you don't think much of me, either."

"Tommy! That is not true!"

"Well, I'm not going to roll over and play dead until you decide all you want from me are my somewhat questionable social skills."

Sabrina got to her feet. "And I never asked you to! Just forget it. Forget I even invited you to the stupid party." She stomped into the house and slammed the door, her chest heaving. How had she managed to pick a fight with easygoing, laid-back Tommy?

For an hour Tommy stared at the computer screen, his concentration shot. What was wrong with him anyway? She'd handed him the perfect opportunity to show him he could fit into her world and he'd blown it. He could have gone with her, been on his best behavior, impressed her friends, and Sabrina would see there was more between them than an unmanageable dog and a ruined flower garden.

He'd let his ego get in the way and argued with her. Way to go, Tommy, he told himself. He'd dug himself a hole so big he'd probably never get out of it.

Skid padded into the room and laid his head on Tommy's knee, glancing up with soulful eyes in commiseration. Tommy ran the palm of his hand across the fur on top of Skid's head. "So what do you think, Skid? My five-year plan's not exactly on track at the moment, is it?"

The doorbell rang. Maybe it was her! He dashed down the hall with Skid at his heels before he remembered he should play it cool with Sabrina. He didn't want to appear too eager. He pulled the door open.

"Yo, Tommy. What's up, man?"

"Hey, Frankie," he answered glumly. He stepped back and held the door open.

"You're not ready."

"For?"

"Pickup basketball. At the park? We play every Wednesday. Remember?"

"Oh, yeah. Right." Tommy tried to work up to his normal level of enthusiasm.

"You sick?" Frankie followed him into the kitchen.

"No." Tommy handed him a bottle of his favorite orange soda and withdrew a ginger ale for himself.

"Hey, you know that friend of your neighbor's? Elaine? She invited me to a party the school principal is giving. Cool, huh?"

"Yeah," Tommy agreed. "Cool."

"She's really nice. When I took her home the other night, she invited me in for coffee. We ended up talking the whole night. Too bad that Sabrina's such a stick-in-the-mud."

"She's not a stick-in-the-mud. Who told you that?"

Frankie held his hands up in self-defense. "Hey, lighten up, man. I just assumed, well, from what Elaine said—"

"Elaine's supposed to be Sabrina's friend. Why is she talking about her behind her back?"

Frankie shook his head, his puzzled gaze never leaving Tommy. "She wasn't talking bad about her. She just told me she hoped Sabrina could find a date to this party because last year some guy had just dumped her and the principal embarrassed her by asking everyone if they knew someone she could go out with."

Tommy stared at Frankie as if he'd just sucker punched him.

"Sabrina's not bad looking or anything. I don't know why no one wants to go out with her. Unless it's her personality."

"There's nothing wrong with her personality," Tommy assured him. *Nothing that can't be fixed, anyway.*

"Oh, well." Frankie brightened. "Maybe she'll ask you to go. We can hang out together."

"Yeah. Maybe." Tommy's earlier gloominess returned in double force.

"Frankie, would you mind if I took a rain check on our game tonight? I've got something I have to do."

Frankie slid off the stool near the counter. "Sure. No problem."

Tommy slid the palms of his hands down the sides of his jeans before he rang Sabrina's doorbell. He heard the chime echo through the house and then the sound of footsteps.

She opened the door dressed in her workout clothes.

"Hi," he said.

She regarded him with frost in her lavender-blue eyes.

"I didn't call you."

"Aw, Bree, come on—"

"No. You're the one who implied I treat you no better than I would a dog—"

"I didn't mean it."

"Yes, you did." Sabrina blinked. She bit her bottom lip. "And I'm afraid you were right. I haven't been very nice to you. I've been judgmental and critical—"

"But in a good way."

"Tommy, you don't owe me anything. And I don't deserve your understanding. Or, I'm afraid, your friendship."

"I'll go to the party with you."

"You don't have to do that."

"I want to. I haven't been to a party in oh, let's see, it's been close to a week, I'd say."

That got a smile out of her and Tommy figured he was gaining ground. "Come on. It'll be fun. I'll behave myself."

"I don't want you to feel like you have to behave!"

"You want me to misbehave? In front of all your friends?"

Sabrina rubbed her temples with the tips of her fingers. "Tommy. Stop. Please. This is exhausting."

"Are we going to the party?"

"Yes. If you insist."

"Cool." He leaned over and turned her wrist so he could see the time on her watch. "So what do you say? Isn't it about time for tea and strumpets? Uh—I mean, crumpets?"

Sabrina chuckled. "Sorry. I'm fresh out of strumpets."

"Aw, darn." Tommy assumed a crestfallen expression.

But there was a mischievous gleam in Sabrina's eyes. "I have some snack cakes, though."

"Snack cakes? You don't mean . . . ?"

Sabrina nodded. "Those yummy yellow sponge cakes with the white filling inside."

Tommy ruffled the hair at the back of her head. "Sabrina Talbott, I do believe there's hope for you yet." He offered her his arm. "Shall we?"

Sabrina's nerves were on edge as she dressed for the party on Saturday. She'd nearly stepped over the line once or twice and asked Tommy what he planned to wear. What if he wore something completely inappropriate or committed some unforgivable faux pas? What was worse? Showing up with no date, or arriving with one who clearly didn't belong? She'd never live it down. Not after last year's fiasco.

She donned a pale turquoise sundress and straw-wedge espadrilles. For once her hair refused to cooperate. Must be the humidity, she decided, as the ends defied their usual tendency to curl under.

She pulled the unmanageable mess into a bunch at the back of her head and secured it with a clip. A few droopy strands hung unenthusiastically around her temples, ears and nape.

She moved on to apply her makeup. What was this? She stared in horror at her mirror. A pimple?

She leaned closer to examine the pale pink bump on her chin. How could this be? Her complexion never broke out!

Cream-filled sponge cakes? Chocolate? Sugary soda? Her conscience asked. *Potato chips? Pizza?*

"Oh, shut up." The blemish seemed to grow in size the

longer she examined it. The pressure from her exploring fingers made the entire area blotchy and more noticeable.

Cover stick. Somewhere she had one. She dug through her makeup drawer searching for it. The clock was ticking. Finally, there it was, buried at the back. She slammed the door shut with a bit too much force. It popped back out and hit her hand.

"Oh, no!" She stared at the broken nail of her previously perfect manicure.

Sabrina wanted to cry, but she had no time. Anxiously she filed the broken nail with an emery board. She could fix the polish. Maybe no one would notice.

As she cleared a place on the narrow bathroom counter the bottle of liquid makeup tipped over. "Oh, no!" she wailed as she retrieved it from the floor. A trail of pinky beige liquid dribbled down the front of the full-skirted sundress and onto her shoes.

In her haste to grab a towel she knocked over the nail polish as well. Pale pink color spattered across the counter.

Tears sprang to Sabrina's eyes. She couldn't repair the dress. She couldn't even repair her broken fingernail. Her ugly pimple was now the size of a pea. The clip in her hair chose that moment to spring loose, tumbling the wayward locks down to her chin.

With a handful of tissues, she hastily cleaned up the nail polish and makeup spills.

Defeated, she stripped off the dress and the shoes. Could she simply not show at the Stricklands' party? Downstairs the doorbell rang. Tommy!

Her panic doubled. She was a wreck. She couldn't deal with him too, especially if he was unsuitably attired.

She pulled on her bathrobe and knotted it around her waist. Tommy's back was to her when she opened the door.

But then he turned around and her heart stopped. Literally stopped.

Sabrina couldn't breathe. She could only stare at Tommy Cameron. Her neighbor from next door. The one with the unruly dog and partying lifestyle. Irresponsible, immature Tommy.

He wore a black polo shirt and khaki trousers. And he was wearing real shoes. His hair was combed. In fact it looked like he'd even had it cut. He held a big bouquet of flowers out to her.

Her mouth dropped open. "You're—you're *perfect*."

"And early apparently," Tommy replied with a grin. His gaze swept over her and then he glanced at his watch. "You did say 5:30, didn't you?"

Sabrina nodded and closed her mouth. She backed up a step so he could enter. He held the flowers out to her again.

"These are for you."

Tears filled Sabrina's eyes at Tommy's thoughtfulness. "Oh, Tommy." Somehow the effort he'd gone to made her feel even worse about her own dishabille.

"What?" asked Tommy anxiously. "You don't like them? Lilies and daffodils? And, hmmm, I forget what the florist said these were. Bird of paradise?"

Sabrina shook her head. "No. Tommy, they're beautiful." She took them from him and the tears spilled over.

"Bree? What's wrong?"

"Nothing. Nothing." How could she explain to Tommy that even though he was so wrong for her, he somehow kept doing all the right things? Making her laugh, cooking for her, bringing her flowers, *getting a haircut*.

"I'm a wreck," she said by way of explanation. He followed her into the kitchen and watched while she found a vase and filled it with water at the sink.

She sniffed and sighed, trying to get hold of herself.

Tommy slid his arms around her from behind. "Bree, what's the matter? What did I do?"

Sabrina shook her head. "Nothing, it's not you. I told you, you're perfect. I'm—I'm—not," she finished awkwardly.

"So who says you have to be perfect all the time?" Tommy asked, his lips brushing her hair.

Sabrina lowered the bouquet into the water and turned. "Look at this." She pointed to the blemish on her chin. "And this." She held up her broken nail. "And this." She grabbed a fistful of limp hair.

"And this." She indicated her robe and bare feet. "I spilled makeup on my dress and nail polish on my shoes."

"I find this," he picked up her hand and kissed the fingertip with the broken nail, "and this," his lips brushed the tiny bump on her chin, "and this," he ran his fingers through her hair, "very appealing."

Sabrina thrust out her lower lip. "You do not."

"And as for this," he tugged on the belt of her bathrobe, "this is a definite turn-on."

"It is not," Sabrina insisted, trying not to smile.

"Let's face it, Sabrina, neither one of us is perfect."

Sabrina nodded, mesmerized by the glint in the depths of his eyes.

"But that doesn't mean we can't go to the party and have a good time, does it?"

Sabrina dropped her gaze. "I don't want to embarrass you," she admitted.

"You don't have to be perfect, Sabrina. No one expects

it of you. Maybe it's time you stopped expecting it of yourself."

"Are you sure you still want to go to the party with me?"

"I'm sure. Now go get dressed."

"Give me ten minutes."

Chapter Fourteen

"Introduce me as Tom, not Tommy," Tommy told Sabrina when he parked near the Strickland home.

"Why? You're Tommy. Everybody calls you Tommy."

"No. You were right that day at Red's. Tommy's a name for a kid. And I'm not a kid anymore." He opened his door and came around to open Sabrina's.

"But Tommy—"

"If you want me to come when I'm called, then the name is Tom. Okay?"

The last thing Sabrina wanted to do was pick another fight with Tommy. Tom. She wasn't sure how they'd managed to make up after the last one. Sharing sponge cakes filled with cream must have had something to do with it, though.

Frank Long and Elaine were already among the guests in the backyard. Clusters of uncharacteristically gaily clad staff and their significant others were scattered around the patio, the brick enclosed barbecue area, and at nearby tables.

Sabrina breathed a sigh of relief, her flagging self-confidence bolstered by Tommy at her side. She knew she wasn't looking her best, although she'd managed to gather her hair into a presentable topknot and touch up the polish on her broken fingernail.

She'd covered the bump on her chin as best she could, although she was sure the blemish was glaringly obvious.

Her damaged sundress had been replaced by a short corduroy jumper over a white T-shirt.

The principal and his wife were standing near the patio doors greeting guests. Sabrina made the appropriate introductions. Tommy passed muster admirably, and Sabrina wondered why she had worried. Hadn't Tommy, in spite of his loud parties, questionable taste in friends, and uncontrollable dog always been a perfect gentleman? How had she overlooked that? Too busy finding fault, she supposed.

"Hello there, you two." Elaine grinned at Sabrina and gave her a knowing smile.

"Hi, Elaine. Frank." Sabrina nodded at Elaine's escort. Another wave of discomfort settled over her. What might Elaine have let slip to Frank about Sabrina's interest in Tommy? And what portion of those shared secrets might Frank pass along to Tommy? If he hadn't already?

"What would you like to drink, Sabrina?" Tommy asked.

"Oh—uh, a diet soda, if they have any. Thanks, Tommy. Uh—Tom."

Tommy and Frank sauntered off together to the makeshift bar.

Sabrina leaned closer to Elaine. "I hope you haven't said anything to Frank about Tommy and me."

Elaine's eyes widened in innocence. "What would I say? That you're crazy about the guy, even though you don't want to admit it?"

"Elaine!" Sabrina hissed.

"Oh, stop it. Do you think Frankie's blind? Do you think any of Tommy's friends are? They already know he's just as crazy about you."

"Really?" Sabrina's mouth dropped open in surprise.

Elaine nodded. "Where have you been? You're Tommy's new girl as far as that crowd is concerned."

"But—but, I just met him two weeks ago."

Elaine shrugged. "That doesn't seem to matter." She smiled as she spotted Frank and Tommy returning with their drinks. "I've only known Frankie for a week. And I'm his new girl."

Sabrina accepted her soft drink from Tommy and couldn't think of a single thing to say other than thank-you. Not even a monosyllabic sentence came to mind. Not that the other three appeared to notice. Tommy and Frankie kept up a running commentary on the baseball playoffs. Frankie draped an arm around Elaine's shoulders. Elaine seemed content to gaze at him adoringly and listen to their male banter.

Is this how falling in love happens, Sabrina wondered, feeling thunderstruck as she watched the two of them. *In only a week or two? Or less?*

Another couple drifted over and joined the group. Introductions were made. The men talked baseball. Elaine and a fellow teacher chatted.

Sabrina's gaze moved to Tommy, er, *Tom.* He looked completely comfortable among her peers. He gestured occasionally with one hand, listened intently when one of the other men made a comment, sipped his drink.

That smile. Those eyes. That incredible body.

Sabrina clamped her lips together as her mouth watered. Tommy's gaze clashed with hers and she swallowed. Her mouth went dry.

He had that glint in his eyes. Not the warm, sleepy, laid-back look. The hot, intense interest in something besides baseball conversation look. Sabrina felt heat creep up her spine. If his eyes could talk, they'd be saying, "I want you."

She wondered what her eyes were saying.

She looked away. Grabbing Elaine's arm, she interrupted her conversation. "Look." She pointed. "There's Stan Mc-Pherson. Let's go say hi. Excuse us?" she asked the others in the group.

"What is with you?" Elaine asked in irritation as they crossed the yard. "You hardly know Stan."

"Isn't that what parties are for? To make new friends?" Sabrina asked brightly. Her knees were shaking. She knew she wasn't acting like her usual self. Shook up. That's how she felt. That's how Tommy—Tom Cameron made her feel.

Tommy stared at his reflection in the bathroom mirror while he dried his hands. He was thirty-two years old, but he felt sixteen with a crush on the girl of his dreams.

Sabrina kept *looking* at him. She'd hardly said a word all evening while he chatted up a storm, trying to show her, he supposed, that he could blend in with her world. The whole time, though, awareness of her hummed through his system like electricity through a wire. After the party, he was going to get her alone and they were going to settle some things between them.

As he passed the staircase on his way back to the party he noticed a boy of perhaps ten or twelve sitting on the third step, dejectedly tossing a football into the air and catching it.

Tommy paused. "Hey, kid."

The boy regarded him without enthusiasm. "Hi." He continued to toss the ball up and down, up and down.

"What's the problem? No one to play with?"

The kid shrugged. "Usually I play with Ben down the street, but he's on vacation. Team tryouts are next week and some of the guys are getting together at Randy Smith's house, but Mom and Dad said I have to stay here." He jerked his head in the direction of the rear of the house. "You know, because of their party."

"Bummer, huh?" Tommy stuck his hand out. "I'm Tommy—uh, Tom."

The boy shook his hand. "I'm Nathan."

Tommy eyed the football which had temporarily ceased motion. "So you want to toss around a few?"

Nathan's eyes lit up. "Really? You wanna? I could really use the practice."

"Sure, why not? Just for awhile."

Tommy stopped at the table. Sabrina still had that look in her eye. Good thing he'd found Nathan. He needed a temporary distraction. Otherwise he might make a scene by tossing Sabrina over his shoulder and taking her home before she was ready to leave. She'd never forgive him for that.

She smiled up at him before she glanced at Nathan. "I see you've made another new friend."

"This is Nathan. We're just going to toss his football around for awhile. If that's okay?" For Pete's sake. What was he doing? Asking her permission? To play football?

What was wrong with him? It wasn't like they were married or anything. He didn't need her to tell him what he could and could not do. He was a free spirit. His own man. And a single one at that. He didn't need a woman's approval or permission to play football with a kid.

Was it his imagination or did Sabrina's grin widen? What was funny?

"Sure, go ahead. You don't need my permission."

Tommy nodded. It was a good thing she understood that.

"Wait, I'll come with you," Frankie said. He glanced at Elaine. "You don't mind, do you?"

Elaine waved him off. "Certainly not. Go ahead."

Frankie dropped a kiss on her lips and squeezed her hand. The three of them loped across the yard, the boy and his new friends. Or was it the *boys* and their new friend?

One thing Sabrina liked about the Stricklands' parties was spending time with Rita Strickland. Warm and sociable, she enjoyed entertaining, and her parties invariably ended up with the women gathered in the kitchen helping her store leftover food and tidying up.

Once the dessert buffet was ready and coffee was made, Sabrina excused herself to the powder room.

How cute had Tommy been coming toward her with Nathan Strickland tagging along behind him? Leave it to Tommy to find the one kid at an adult party.

Not that Tommy, er, Tom, hadn't made a good impression on the assembled adults as well. Sabrina had to admit to herself that Tommy Cameron was neither irresponsible nor immature. Contrary to her earlier impressions, he was well-read, intelligent, and possessed impeccable manners.

A couple of the women had quizzed her about him, peppering their questions with positive comments.

"Good looking and a brain too. Where did you find him?" Delia Potter wanted to know.

"I can't believe you found a guy who's actually heard of feng shui," Valerie Cooper gushed. "Does he have any single friends?"

Maybe I'll have a party, Sabrina mused. *Invite all of Tommy's friends to meet mine.*

Huh? Sabrina stared at her reflection. A party? *Her?* What could she be thinking?

She put her lipstick away and continued her internal conversation on her way back outside. *If her friends liked Tommy, then why wouldn't they like Tommy's friends too? Look at Elaine and Frank. Look at Tommy and me.*

Yes, look. She found Tommy behind Nathan Strickland who was hunched forward, ready to hike the ball. And it looked like every guy at the party had taken sides. They were all playing touch football. Even some of the women had joined the game. The rest of the guests cheered from the sidelines.

Nathan hiked the ball. Tommy stepped back, looking to throw. His gaze collided with Sabrina's. He hesitated as if frozen in motion, oblivious to the shouts of the others to pass the ball. Too late. Tommy went down. Tackled behind the line of scrimmage.

Sabrina, who knew very little about football, cheered.

Chapter Fifteen

Sabrina was quiet on the way home. Too quiet, Tommy thought.

He shouldn't have started that football game with the principal's kid. He should have behaved like an adult and ignored the boy.

Instead the male guests, in their stylish casual pleated shorts and neatly pressed short-sleeved shirts and loafers worn without socks had joined him and Nathan on the lawn. They'd all ended up hot and sweaty and grass-stained.

Tommy could have sworn they were having a good time. Some of the guests made up cheerleading routines along the sidelines.

Finally everyone trooped back in for dessert and a cold drink. Then the party broke up.

And Sabrina hadn't said a word on the drive home.

He'd let her down. Embarrassed her in front of her boss and her colleagues. He'd probably blown any chance he'd had of showing her that he might be her type.

"I'm sorry, Bree." He parked the Jeep in front of his house, jammed the gearshift into neutral, and engaged the parking brake.

Sabrina turned toward him. "Pardon me. What did you say?"

So she was really going to make him suffer.

"I said I'm sorry," he sputtered. It was bad enough saying those words once. And to a woman no less. But to have to repeat it. Oh man!

"Sorry? About what?"

Tommy sighed. He released his seat belt and tapped his fingers on the steering wheel. "For ruining the party. Making you look bad."

"Tommy!"

He held up a hand. "I know. I know. Playing football was a bad idea. Very immature."

"Tommy." Sabrina laid her hand on his forearm.

He couldn't look at her. "I'm sorry I embarrassed you."

"What are you talking about? You didn't embarrass me."

Tommy chanced a quick look her way. "I didn't?"

"Of course not. Principal Strickland's guests had fun at his party tonight. And it was all because of you."

"Are you sure?"

"Tommy, trust me. You were the life of the party."

"I was?"

"Aren't you always?"

"I thought you were mad at me."

"Why?"

"Because you haven't said a word since we left the party."

"Oh. I was thinking, that's all."

Tommy came around to her side and opened the door. "Thinking about what?"

You. "Oh, I don't know. Everything and nothing," Sabrina hedged as they strolled up the walk to her door.

"I can do better," Tommy said. "If you give me another chance."

"Better? What do you mean?"

"I mean I'd really like to go out with you. I know you think I'm not the guy for you, but maybe I could be."

"Tommy—"

"Call me Tom." Tommy insisted.

"Tom." Sabrina had been trying to remind herself all evening to think of Tommy as Tom, but it was next to impossible. The name Tommy suited him whether she wanted to admit it or not. "That'll take some getting used to." She unlocked her door. "Want to come in for coffee?"

"I'm not much of a coffee drinker, unless it's before noon."

Sabrina smiled. "I believe asking one's date in for coffee is a euphemism used by women everywhere to indicate they're not quite ready for the evening to end. *Tom.*"

"Sorry. I'm confused. I didn't think we were on a date." Tommy followed her inside.

I'm glad I'm not the only one who's confused, Sabrina thought. She didn't really want any coffee. She didn't know what she wanted. Except she didn't want Tommy to leave.

"Well, if you don't want coffee, is there anything else you'd like?" Sabrina asked.

To kiss you, Tommy thought.

Whoa. Wait a minute. Tommy remembered his plan just in the nick of time. The plan was to turn himself into the kind of man she thought she wanted. She'd made it clear from the beginning that she didn't like impulsive haven't-got-a-plan-or-a-thought-about-the-future types. She wanted someone more conservative. Not someone who expected a kiss on the first date.

He cleared his throat. "I should probably get going." On the way home he smiled at the memory of the disappointed look on Sabrina's face at his sudden departure.

His plan was going to work. He was sure of it.

Chapter Sixteen

Sabrina returned from church just after noon. She had prayed for patience, even though she'd heard the only way to learn patience was to be tried and tried again.

Perhaps she should have prayed to keep her sanity before Tommy drove her crazy.

She went into the kitchen to make a salad for lunch and plan her afternoon. There's always housework, she thought to herself. Grandma Mamie's antiques were beautiful, but they required a lot of care to keep the wood from drying out and the patina from fading.

While she stood at the sink rinsing tomatoes, music floated through the kitchen window. She leaned forward and peeked out, catching a glimpse of Tommy in his back-yard. He was with Frank Long and Buddy Ellington. Buddy was filling a bucket with water while Tommy and Frank unloaded wood planks from the back of Frank's truck.

Tommy had his shirt off. His muscles gleamed in the bright sunshine. A pair of denim cutoffs rode low on his waist, exposing the top band of his briefs. The cuffs of his socks peeked over the top of ankle-high work boots. He looked absolutely delicious.

She dropped the tomatoes into the colander and dried her hands. Her mouth was dry. And her head, apparently, was empty.

The music came from Frank's truck radio. Something country and twangy.

Tommy and Frank dropped a couple of planks on the pile already accumulated on the grass and turned back to the truck.

She halted just shy of the property line between her domain and Tommy's.

"Hi." As monosyllabic greetings went, it was as good as any, Sabrina decided. Simple. Straightforward. Best of all, it got Tommy's attention.

Tommy's head whipped around. He halted immediately, changed directions, and walked her way.

"Hi yourself." He grinned at her. "What's up?"

She snapped her gaze away from his muscles and back to his face. Huh? What? "Fine."

He continued to stand there and look at her. "I like your dress."

Sabrina gazed down at the flowered cotton shift. Soon she'd have to put it away until next summer. If she didn't melt in the warmth of Tommy's eyes before then. "Thanks."

Frank continued to unload planks of wood.

"What are you guys doing?" Sabrina asked.

"Building a fence." Tommy strolled back toward the truck and Sabrina followed.

"Why?"

He picked up a plank and added it to the growing stack on the ground.

"Because it's the responsible thing to do," Tommy answered.

"It is?"

He ruffled her hair lightly on his way back to the truck. "It is when you have a dog who likes to dig up the neighbor's flowers."

"Oh." Sabrina had always thought of herself as someone with decent conversational skills, but she seemed sadly lacking in them today. She scrambled for something else to say. Something interesting. "I thought I saw Buddy out here."

"He went in to use the phone."

"Oh."

Frank caught her eye and gave her one of those knowing grins. "Hi again, Sabrina."

"Hi, Frank. How are you?"

He grabbed the end of a plank. "Oh, I'm just great. Nothing I like better than getting up early on a Sunday morning to build a fence."

"I'm making it worth your while," Tommy said good-naturedly. He winked at Sabrina.

Sabrina decided right then and there to nominate him for the Sexiest Man of the Year award. She'd offer to be the grand prize.

Tommy dashed the sweat from his brow with his forearm. The truck bed was almost empty.

"Can I get you guys something to drink? Some lemonade?"

"I knew there was a reason I liked you, Sabrina," Frank said.

Tommy elbowed him in the ribs. "Knock it off. She's mine." He winked at Sabrina. *Again.* As if they shared an inside joke. Sabrina felt sure it was a joke she wasn't getting. Still, a thrill went through her at his words. *She's mine.*

"Well, you're sure taking your time figuring that one out," Frank muttered loud enough to be heard by both of them. He picked up the bucket of water Buddy had filled and started to pour cement mix into it.

"I'll go make that lemonade."

Sabrina removed a can of frozen lemonade from her freezer, dumped it into a plastic pitcher, and added water. All the while her brain buzzed with thoughts of Tommy. Tommy with his shirt off. Tommy winking at her. Tommy telling Frank "she's mine."

Yet he hadn't made a move last night when he had the opportunity. He'd sent off mixed messages all evening. The last thing she wanted to do was throw herself at him and have him reject her advances.

After all, as he had pointed out, they weren't exactly on a date to begin with. She'd made it clear she didn't want to date him. Because she thought he was all wrong for her.

Except maybe he wasn't. He apparently had a steady if somewhat unconventional means of earning a living. He had a circle of friends, ones he'd had since childhood. Which meant what? That he was loyal? That he possessed the ability to build lasting relationships? He was doing his best to control his dog. First the obedience training, and now a fence.

Sabrina dug through her cupboards for plastic cups. Had she completely misjudged Tommy from the get-go? Even Elaine had noted Tommy wasn't as irresponsible as Sabrina made him out to be. He *had* apologized for Skid's destructiveness. He *had* replaced her flowers. And he had impressed everyone at the Stricklands' barbecue. The principal had even thanked Tommy for finding a way to include his young son in the adults-only party.

She wanted to tell Tommy all of this. To tell him she'd been wrong in her initial assumptions.

She filled the cups with ice and lemonade and set them on a tray along with the pitcher.

Frank and Tommy were just finishing setting another post into a cement-filled hole. Garth Brooks bellowed from the truck radio. Bright fall sunshine poured down on them.

All Sabrina could see was Tommy's smile of appreciation and the warmth of his eyes as she crossed the grass. Like one of those old hair-color commercials, she imagined herself in slow motion, running through a field toward Tommy, arms outstretched, offering him a cold glass of lemonade to refresh his overheated body. She didn't see Buddy open the back door of Tommy's house. She didn't see Skid bound out and make a beeline toward her.

She was too focused on Tommy, too caught up in the fantasies he inspired. The music muffled the sound of Skid's oversized paws as he barreled in her direction.

Then, like a hair-color commercial gone wrong, Skid, in his mad dash of excitement, knocked into her. Tommy automatically put his arms out to catch her, and that probably would have worked if he hadn't been standing so close to the poles lying beside him.

The heel of his boot caught on the end of one. With his arms already occupied, he lost his balance and landed flat on his back. Sabrina landed on top of him amidst a shower of ice and lemonade. Skid, in his usual manic pattern, continued to dash about the yard as if he'd just invented some wonderful new game.

Sabrina removed herself from Tommy's lemonade-covered chest.

Tommy didn't move.

"Tommy?" She scooted up beside him and searched his face with anxious eyes. His eyes were closed. Frank hunkered down next to him.

"Tom?" He slapped Tommy's cheek. "Wake up, buddy."

Sabrina's gaze flickered from Frank to Tommy. "What's wrong? Why isn't he waking up? What if I killed him?" *What if I never see that smile again? Those eyes? That wink?*

"He's got a pulse and he's breathing. Let's not panic just yet." Frank slapped Tommy's cheek again. "Yo. Tommy. Wake up, would you?"

Sabrina scooted around and cradled Tommy's head in her lap.

"He's got a lump forming back here," she informed the other two.

"Buddy, go get some ice, okay?"

Buddy took off to do Frank's bidding. "You sure don't seem very worried," Sabrina noted.

"He's all right." Frank gazed at Tommy, and she thought he sort of smiled before he moved away.

"Tommy? Tommy?" She smoothed the damp hair back from his forehead and temples.

Skid returned and began gobbling up the spilled ice. The dog swiped his tongue across Tommy's ribs, lapping at the dribbles of lemonade.

Sabrina scowled at Skid. "Tommy, I'm warning you, if you don't wake up, I won't be responsible for what happens to that dog of yours."

She thought she saw Tommy's brow pucker and his lip quirk. She stroked a hand along his jaw. "Tommy? Are you in there?" Gently she slid her thumb along his lower lip. And about had a heart attack when his tongue flicked out and licked it.

"Tommy!"

He opened his eyes and gave her the half-lazy, half-intense look. Then he grinned. "Wow. That must have been some lemonade."

Buddy returned with a plastic bag filled with ice and handed it to a now-suspicious Sabrina. She thought she heard Frank chuckle. Tommy made no move to sit up.

"We thought you were unconscious," she informed Tommy.

"Is that ice for me?"

Sabrina became even more wary when she saw the innocent sparkle in his eyes.

"You've got a nice bump on the back of your head."

"Yeah? Is there any lemonade left?"

Sabrina surveyed the upturned pitcher and scattered cups. A satisfied Skid lay panting in the shade of a lilac bush near Tommy's back porch.

"No, but I can make some more."

"Good." He sat up, muffling a groan, and reached for the ice pack, pressing it to the back of his head.

Sabrina stood and looked down at him, trying to decide if he'd really been out of commission the whole time or not. Buddy had joined Frank and they were studiously setting another post into the ground. There seemed no alternative but to gather up the empty pitcher and cups and make more lemonade.

Chapter Seventeen

Sabrina changed into a T-shirt and shorts since her flowered shift had gotten a bit sticky and grass stained. Her monthly dry-cleaning bill had hit a new high since Tommy and Skid's arrival.

She made sure Skid had been banished back inside the house before she ventured out. Frank, Buddy, and Tommy stopped work long enough to down a couple glasses of lemonade each. Buddy, Sabrina learned, was a supervisor for an overnight delivery service.

He was sort of attractive, and he had a nice smile. Maybe Delia Potter would be interested in meeting him.

Joey Gianetti appeared around the corner of the house and joined the group gathered around Frank's truck. "Sorry I couldn't get here any earlier. Had an emergency. Major surgery on an old lady's plumbing."

"Got her all fixed up, did you, Joe?" Frank asked.

"Oh, yeah, no problem. You know how it is. Those old pipes rust and wear out after fifty or sixty years."

Sabrina poured some lemonade for Joey and handed it to him. She'd met him briefly at the party for Pam. It hadn't occurred to her he had a medical degree. He didn't seem the type. "Are you a doctor, Joe? I had no idea."

Joey choked on his mouthful of lemonade and turned aside just before it spewed forth. The other guys guffawed. Even Tommy chuckled. He shook his head at her.

"What?" Sabrina wanted to know. She fixed her gaze on Joey. "Didn't you just say you performed major surgery on an old lady's pipes?"

This produced even more laughter from the assembled group of men. Sabrina crossed her arms over her chest and frowned.

Frankie dried his eyes and recovered first. "Joey's a plumber."

"A plumber? Oh." Rats. Just when she was starting to think Joey and Valerie Cooper would hit it off. Valerie liked the finer things in life, and a wealthy physician would be in a position to keep her in such a lifestyle. Then Sabrina recalled the outrageous amount her plumber had charged for repairs to her leaky toilet. Maybe she'd introduce Valerie to Joey after all.

The guys set down their empty cups and started back to work. "Anything I can do to help?" she asked Tommy.

"I think you've done enough. Unless you want to kiss this lump on my head and make it better."

"Gladly." Sabrina congratulated herself on managing a two-syllable response and not blushing.

Tommy stood in front of where she was seated on the open gate of the pickup. He placed his hands on either side of her so they were face to face. Their eyes met and held for a moment. Sabrina dropped her gaze to his lips.

He bowed his head and Sabrina could see the raised swelling even before she parted his hair. She gave the bump a soft kiss, breathing in the scent of his sun-warmed hair, the tang of perspiration, and the fainter aromas of grass and dog before he lifted his head. "Better now?"

"Much," he answered, his voice low and husky.

"I bet you guys will be hungry later. I could make you dinner."

"We can always order a pizza."

"How about spaghetti instead? Salad and garlic bread? I'll see if Elaine wants to come over and help me."

"Sounds good. But you don't have to."

"I want to," Sabrina insisted, surprised to find it was true.

Elaine leapt at the chance to help Sabrina cook dinner for Tommy and the guys. She arrived laden with grocery bags and promptly left through the back door to visit Frank Long.

Sabrina smiled and hummed to herself as she went about preparing a spaghetti dinner for six. The country tunes from Frank's truck radio wafted in on the warm breeze. The sound of nails hitting wood and the guys calling back and forth to each other mingled with the music.

An odd sense of contentment washed over her as she set her dining room table. Elaine's question came back to her. "When's the last time you had a man in your house?" Tommy'd been the first one in a long time. And now she was about to add three more.

The guys trooped in just as darkness began to fall, filling Sabrina's house with their male presence. While Elaine poured iced tea, Tommy came up behind Sabrina where she stirred the spaghetti sauce. He looked over her shoulder and sniffed. "Smells good."

"That's the basil and oregano."

"I wasn't talking about the food." He pushed her hair behind her ear and nuzzled her neck. Sabrina got that excited, tingly feeling again.

"Are you hungry?" Even though she managed a complete sentence, her words came out soft and husky.

"Starving," Tommy answered.

"We'll be ready to eat in a minute," she told him, choosing to ignore the possible double meaning of his last response.

He'd washed up and put on a dark blue Notre Dame T-shirt.

"You guys can go sit down and we'll dish it up."

After dinner, as she and Elaine tidied up the kitchen and prepared dessert, Sabrina reflected on the perfect ending to a perfect weekend. Who would have thought?

She'd sat at one end of the dining table and Tommy ended up on the other, which meant they were looking at each other for most of the meal. Elaine and Frank had paired up along one side, Buddy and Joey on the other.

They'd laughed and talked, and Sabrina had felt a sense of belonging such as she'd never felt before. Tommy had somehow managed to fill her house with friends and laughter just as he filled his own. And what's wrong with that? she asked herself. Why do you have such a problem with it? She didn't. Not anymore. Her attitude had done an about-face in a matter of weeks and no one was more surprised than Sabrina.

"I'm thinking of having a party," Sabrina told Elaine as they scooped out ice cream and arranged cookies on a tray.

"A party? You?"

"You don't have to act so surprised," Sabrina admonished her.

Elaine put the lid on the ice cream and returned it to the freezer. "Sorry. I thought you didn't like parties."

"I never used to. But look, Elaine, you met Frank at one. And I sort of met Tommy the same way."

"Mm hmm." Elaine raised an eyebrow. "Your point?"

"Buddy and Joey. Don't you think they'd like to meet Delia and Valerie?"

"Ah, a matchmaking party!"

"Not necessarily." Sabrina laid spoons and extra napkins on the tray. "But Tommy's got a lot of friends."

"And you've got a lot of friends."

"No. I have a lot of acquaintances. But if you and I hit it off with Tommy's crowd, and he and Frank seemed to enjoy the Strickland party—"

"Chances are they all might mix well together?"

"What do you think?"

"I think it's a great idea. I'll even help you."

"Thanks, Elaine. You're a real pal."

"Are you kidding? I owe you big time. If not for you, I'd never have met Frank."

Frank and Elaine were the first to leave. No surprise there, Sabrina decided. Shortly afterward, Buddy and Joey departed, leaving her and Tommy alone. And Sabrina in her usual tongue-tied state.

She nervously finished cleaning up. Tommy sat at the kitchen table. She could feel him tracking her every move.

She finally ran out of things to do and turned toward him, leaning back against the counter.

"How's your head?"

"I'll live." He held out a hand to her. "Come here."

Sabrina took his hand and he tugged her down to his lap

and wrapped his arms around her, burying his face in her hair. "I've been wanting to do this all day."

"You—you have?" Sabrina felt surrounded, enveloped by Tommy's warmth, the sincerity of his words.

"Hmmm." He cupped her head in his hands and kissed her. Sabrina slid her arms around his neck and returned his kiss, until slowly, deliberately, he ended it and unlocked her arms. Sabrina didn't even try to hold back her expression of dismay. Slowly she opened her eyes. Tommy's glittered down at her.

"Why'd you stop?"

"Because I don't want to start something I can't finish. And I don't want you to jump into something that's not right for you."

"What do you mean?"

"It wasn't so long ago you had yourself convinced I wasn't your type."

"But that was before I knew you," Sabrina protested.

"I haven't changed that much in two weeks, Sabrina."

Sabrina bit her lip. She knew more of her words were going to come back to haunt her. "Is this because of what I said about living next door to each other?"

Tommy smoothed her hair. "That's part of it."

"What's the rest of it?"

"I don't think you know what you want."

"Yes, I do. Or I did. I thought I did." *Until you came along and turned my world upside down.*

He smiled. "When you figure it out, I hope you'll let me know. Neighbor."

"I guess this means you're going home now."

"Yeah. I guess." But Tommy leaned in for one last kiss before he let her go.

Sabrina really didn't know what she wanted. She wanted

Tommy to stay. But in the face of his reluctance to take their relationship a step further, she decided to save face and let him go.

"Want to go to obedience training with me tomorrow?" he asked, once they were on the porch.

Sabrina was beginning to wonder just who was training whom. The classes were supposed to be for Skid, but Skid was the least of her concerns now. She'd thought maybe she could train Tommy to be the man of her dreams, but lately it didn't seem like he needed much in the way of training. Maybe she was the one benefiting the most from those classes. Because it meant she got to spend time with Tommy.

"I'd love to."

"Pizza first?"

Sabrina didn't even think twice about the caloric content of pizza. "Sounds good."

Tommy gave her another quick kiss and stepped off the porch. "See you tomorrow, then."

Sabrina watched him saunter back to his house.

He loves me. He loves me not. He loves me.

Definitely have to plant some daisies, she thought.

Chapter Eighteen

Tuesday morning Sabrina woke feeling a bit sluggish. *Too much pizza last night,* she reminded herself. Ah, but it was such fun sharing a pizza with Tommy, drinking regular soda, feeding the crusts to Skid.

Having fun. The idea no longer scared her. With Tommy it felt normal and natural. Maybe this is what her mother found so attractive about her stepfather. It was okay to be yourself instead of the person you thought others expected you to be. After the past couple of weeks in Tommy's company, Sabrina was starting to believe anything was possible.

She donned her running shorts, tank top, and sneakers, grabbed her hand weights, and set off. Another reason she liked the location of her house was its proximity to the country roads that led out of town. Mostly deserted, they offered a perfect blend of solitude and scenery.

She'd gone less than a mile when she heard footsteps behind her. One glance over her shoulder told her Tommy and Skid were also out for some exercise, though they both moved at a comfortable jog.

When it seemed Tommy had had sufficient time to overtake her, but hadn't, Sabrina looked back once again. He was about ten feet behind her. His pace had slowed considerably and he showed no signs of speeding up.

She turned around and walked backwards to ask, "Why'd you slow down?"

"So I could admire the scenery." He had that mischievous grin on his face and the now-familiar glint in his eyes. His meaning was all too clear. He certainly hadn't been concentrating on the cornfields, barns, and occasional clusters of grazing cattle.

"Pervert." Sabrina turned around and added some extra wiggle to her hips, smiling to herself.

Tommy caught up to her and gave a lock of her hair a playful tug. With his long stride, he didn't have to work very hard to keep pace with her.

She raised an eyebrow at him. "Getting hot back there?"

"Uh-huh. It's not easy keeping up with you."

Again, Sabrina had that feeling there was a double meaning in his words.

"I didn't know you jogged."

Tommy glanced at his watch. "I decided to take it up about twenty minutes ago."

Sabrina picked up on what he wasn't saying. She'd passed his house about twenty minutes ago.

Skid bounded ahead, stopping to sniff in the weeds and wildflowers that grew along either side of the pavement. "Skid seems to be enjoying himself," Sabrina commented.

"Hang on. I'll show you something." He stopped and Sabrina did too.

"Skid. Come." Skid paused in his antics, unburied his nose from the weeds about twenty feet ahead, and looked back at Tommy.

"Skid. Come." Tommy repeated, increasing the level of command in his voice.

Skid bounded back to Tommy and halted when Tommy put a hand out, palm down, in front of the dog's face.

"Skid, sit." Skid complied, his eyes seeking approval, tongue lolling out of his mouth.

"Good dog. Okay, come here." Tommy hunkered down and scratched Skid's chest with one hand. From his shorts pocket he took a dog treat which Skid gobbled in one bite. Then they turned twin pairs of brown eyes on Sabrina.

That did it. If Sabrina hadn't been in love before, she fell hard right then for the boy and his dog. "Wow," she managed, her voice so suddenly clogged with emotion she had trouble speaking. "You've really been working with him. I'm impressed."

Tommy grinned, ruffled Skid's fur, and stood. "Okay!" he said, and Skid bounded off once again. He looked at Sabrina. "He's not as dumb as he looks. He just needed someone to show him the way is all."

Sabrina stood there, looking at Tommy, knowing he was trying to tell her something that had nothing to do with Skid's obedience training. "Maybe we all need to be shown how to do things differently." She hoped Tommy would understand she was including herself in that statement.

The three of them returned home in companionable silence, Sabrina to her house, Tommy and Skid to theirs. Sabrina showered and went downstairs to have breakfast.

Still in her bathrobe, she stepped outside to get the newspaper and halted in surprise. A huge van sat in front of

Tommy's house. As she watched, two men came down the porch steps carrying Tommy's Naugahyde sofa.

Tommy wasn't leaving, was he? He'd just moved in! That's what free spirits do, Sabrina, she reminded herself. They flit from place to place. You can't tie them down. But surely he'd have said something to her about it? Wouldn't he have?

He loves me.

He loves me not.

Sabrina bounded off the porch and marched across the two lawns, her concentration on Tommy, who stood with his back to her watching the sofa's progress. She'd spent so much time gazing at him the past week or two, by now she even recognized him from behind. Except he wasn't in his usual jeans and T-shirt.

"Tommy?"

She skidded to an abrupt halt when Tommy lifted his head and turned around. "Howdy, neighbor. Long time, no see." His gaze swept her bathrobe and damp hair. "Nice outfit."

Sabrina clutched her robe more tightly around herself. "You too." She felt immensely proud of herself for managing that simple response since she was in shock. Again.

Tommy wore a pair of black trousers and a long-sleeved white shirt with the sleeves rolled back. His damp hair was slicked back from his forehead. The business-casual look threw her off. And turned her on.

"Wow, Tommy. You're all dressed up." She eyed the maroon and gray striped tie draped around his neck. "Almost."

"I've got a meeting with a new client this morning. What's up?"

That explained his clothes, but it didn't explain the van

in front of his house or the sofa heading toward it. "Are— are you moving?" Sabrina didn't know what she'd do if he said yes. Cry? Scream? Throw herself at his feet and beg him to stay?

"No. Just having some new furniture delivered." He nodded back to the truck where the same two men were now unloading a navy blue leather sofa. Even through the plastic covering it, Sabrina could see the quality of the piece.

"Nice," she murmured. Tommy held what looked like delivery tickets in his hand.

"Yeah," Tommy agreed. "That other sofa was pretty beat up. Pam helped me pick out the new stuff. She's an interior decorator."

"She is?"

"Yeah. That's one of the reasons she came to visit after I bought the house."

"Oh." *Now who's slow on the uptake,* Sabrina wondered. She really had to learn to stop making snap judgments about people. Especially since they were so often inaccurate.

Tommy's old sofa now sat near the truck, looking lost and unneeded.

She gazed at it with longing. "But your old couch looked so. . . ." Well-worn? Informal? "Comfortable?"

Tommy looked at her oddly. "I hope the kids at the youth center appreciate it as much as you. It's going in the rec room down there."

Tommy was donating his old couch to a worthwhile nonprofit organization. What a grown-up thing to do.

Sabrina bit her lip, more confused than ever. "Well, I better go get dressed."

"Are you sure? I kind of like you just the way you are." One corner of Tommy's mouth quirked up in a grin.

"Me too." Sabrina found herself melting in the warmth of his eyes. Sentences, Sabrina, she scolded herself. With bigger words. Make him understand. "Uh, that is, I mean, I like you too. Just the way you are." Okay. Long sentences with lots of small words. Almost as good.

She backed away a couple of steps, anxious for a quick retreat before she started babbling like a baby. She made it back to her house and inside the door. Then she remembered her newspaper was still lying on the walk.

When she arrived home around five, she was smiling. She'd had a good day. Maybe every day is a good day when you're in love. She had no real experience in that area before now.

She'd begun her introduction to Victorian poetry and engaged the students in a lively discussion of Elizabeth Barrett Browning's sonnets. "How do I love thee? Let me count the ways."

I love your eyes. Your fun-loving ways. Your friends. Your music. Your muscles. The way you stand in your bedroom at night in your pajama bottoms and brush your teeth while you watch TV. I love your dog, and the way he digs up my flowers. I love every pair of jeans and every single T-shirt you own.

Several times, Sabrina had had to pull herself out of her own personal musings to keep the discussion on track.

I love the way you kiss. And the way you call crumpets muffets. Or strumpets. And the way you take an interest in a bored kid and turn an adult party into a free-for-all football game complete with cheerleaders. In short, Tommy Cameron, I think I love just about everything about you.

Sabrina started up her walk with a spring in her step. She glanced next door and did a double take. Tommy was on the front steps, swabbing a paintbrush back and forth. She set her things down near her door and crossed the lawn to investigate.

"You've been busy," she said as she approached.

Tommy wore a Chicago Cubs baseball cap backwards, and he was back in ancient jeans and a T-shirt, both spattered here and there with pearly gray paint.

"Hi, Bree." He sat back on his haunches and looked at her. "Yeah, the porch floor was pretty worn. Been meaning to paint it ever since I moved in."

Sabrina looked at the fresh coat of paint. "Looks good." Something else on the far side of the porch caught her attention, and she walked past Tommy to see what it was.

"A trellis?" she marveled.

"Noticed it at the hardware store while I was buying paint. Figured I'd hang it at that end of the porch. Get some kind of plant with vines and put it there. Got any ideas?"

"Climbing roses would be pretty. As long as you can keep Skid away from them."

Tommy swabbed his brush along the bottom step. "His digging days are over."

Sabrina supposed that meant Skid wouldn't be digging up any more of her roses. Or hydrangeas. And she couldn't look forward to shopping for new ones with Tommy. Stopping for ribs and root beer on the way home. Returning from work to find him hard at work planting them.

"Where is Skid, anyway?"

"Out back. Where he belongs."

Well, dogs had been known to dig under fences. Maybe there was hope for Skid yet.

Tommy recapped the paint can, laid his brush on top, and wiped his hands on a rag.

"Hey, Bree, I've got some stuff I gotta get done this

week, but would you maybe like to go to dinner on Saturday?"

"You mean like a date?" Sabrina smiled at the thought.

"Yeah. If you're up for it."

But wait a minute. Tommy, typical male that he was, had been sending her mixed messages. Maybe he hadn't figured out what he wanted either. Which was too bad since she now knew exactly what she wanted. Potential heartbreak loomed directly in front of her.

"I'll think about it."

Tommy blinked. "You'll think about it?"

"I'm not just some poodle you can lead around by the rhinestone collar, you know."

"I never said you were. Are we going to have another fight?"

"That depends. I don't want you to think you can just snap your fingers and I'll come running. You told me the other night I didn't know what I wanted. But maybe you don't either. You didn't want to start something you couldn't finish. You don't want to jump into something that isn't right for you."

"Look, Sabrina, if you don't want to go out with me, just say so."

"I do."

"Then why are you giving me such a hard time?"

In the face of Tommy's exasperation, Sabrina had to ask herself the same question. Because a real date seemed like the official start of something. Something big. Something serious and terrifying. Like falling madly, deeply in love with Tommy and never looking back.

She couldn't tell him all of that, though. Maybe if she agreed to dinner he wouldn't notice that she didn't answer his question. "I'm up for it. I'll look forward to it."

"Good. Dress up. I want to take you somewhere nice."

There didn't seem to be anything else to say. "So I'll see you Saturday?"

Tommy nodded. "Around seven?"

Chapter Nineteen

Sabrina hardly saw Tommy over the next few days, but she noticed subtle changes around his house, and occasionally she heard hammering from his backyard.

In addition to his porch floor and steps, the trim now had a fresh coat of white paint. The trellis hung at one end of his porch ready for spring and the planting of climbing roses. Sabrina would be more than happy to help him pick them out. She'd even offer to plant them.

She went through her wardrobe trying to decide what to wear for her date with Tommy. Something nice. Something sexy, Sabrina decided. Something not her usual conservative style. Nothing in her closet fit the bill.

She spent two evenings scouring Oglethorpe's better department stores until finally she found the perfect dress. Long-sleeved and black, it had a scooped neckline, and it clung to her curves like nobody's business. "Oh, yeah!"

she commented to her reflection in the dressing room mirror. Her eyes sparkled, and she couldn't wipe the smile off her face. "Tommy Cameron, you are mine."

She found strappy black heels within her budget in the shoe department.

On Friday she had her hair trimmed and splurged on a manicure and a pedicure. Saturday was going to be perfect. She couldn't wait.

When Sabrina answered her door promptly at seven Saturday night, she knew she looked her absolute best. No ugly pimples, no broken nails. Her hair had cooperated with her efforts as usual.

Nothing she'd seen thus far in Tommy Cameron's repertoire of tricks to keep her off balance and guessing, however, could have prepared her for the sight which greeted her.

Tommy filled out a dark blue pinstriped suit the same way he did T-shirts and jeans. The jacket had been tailored perfectly to fit his tall, broad-shouldered frame. Sabrina tried not to gape at the snowy white dress shirt with a button-down collar and the Windsor knotted burgundy tie. Black wing tips polished to a high gloss completed his man-about-town look. In his hand he held one perfect long-stemmed red rose. He offered it to her as she stood there, agape at his transformation. If she wasn't mistaken, he'd gotten yet another haircut, making his previously unruly locks a thing of the past.

He smiled and Sabrina knew on some level it was the Tommy smile of old, but she couldn't quite connect it with the man standing in front of her.

"Tommy?" she queried, in definite need of reassurance

that Tommy didn't have an investment banker identical twin.

"You can call me Tom. Or Thomas. Tommy's kind of a childish name for a grown man, don't you think?"

"I—uh—if you say so." Tommy was throwing her own words of a few weeks ago back at her. Unfortunately, his agreement with her was about two weeks too late, for, like a typical woman, she'd done an about-face and decided Tommy suited him far better than Tom or, God forbid, *Thomas* ever would.

Thomas stepped across the threshold and Sabrina sniffed the delicate rose, trying to think of something more to say.

"You look nice," he told her.

Nice? *Nice!* She knew for a fact she looked way better than nice. She was dressed to kill. She looked dynamite. And boy did she ever want him to acknowledge this was so. Two could play his game, though. She'd show him!

"Thanks. So do you."

"Are you ready to go then?"

Let the games begin. "Sure am." Sabrina picked up her evening bag.

Tommy led her to the curb where a four-door luxury sedan was parked. He clicked a remote control to unlock it and opened the door. Sabrina hesitated. She glanced at the other cars parked on the street. "Where's your Jeep?"

"It's a rather impractical vehicle for a grown man with responsibilities, don't you think?" He helped her in and closed the door.

Sabrina took note of the plush leather seats as she fastened her seatbelt. Had Tommy traded in his Jeep? No more rides with the wind blowing through her hair? No more sense of freedom that came from riding in the open vehicle?

She glanced up as Tommy slid into the driver's seat. At least this car had a sunroof.

"So you got rid of the Jeep and you bought this?"

"You don't like it?"

"It's not that, it's just that. . . ." *It's not you. It's too practical. Too conservative. Too Thomas.* "Could you open the sunroof?"

Tommy steered the car away from the curb. "Aren't you afraid the wind will mess up your hair?"

Sabrina shook her head. "No. But maybe you're afraid it will mess up yours." She eyed his severe haircut.

Tommy opened the sunroof. *Not as good as the Jeep,* Sabrina decided, *but it will have to do.*

"I made reservations at the Red Door Inn in Maple Grove, by the way."

"The Red Door? Wow." Sabrina knew for a fact the Red Door Inn in nearby Maple Grove was the classiest restaurant within a hundred miles. She'd never been there, but she knew it was expensive. The food was rumored to be excellent and there was live entertainment on Friday and Saturday nights.

"I hope that's okay with you." Tommy's gaze flickered her way before he concentrated once again on driving, both hands on the wheel at ten o'clock and two o'clock.

Not as good as the ribs at Red's probably. Or a sundae at the Frosty Freeze. "I'm sure it will be very nice."

They managed polite conversation on the half-hour drive to Maple Grove. Sabrina tried to quell her sense of growing dismay. The lighthearted, free-spirited Tommy she'd come to know and love seemed to have disappeared behind the serious and proper Thomas facade. She didn't like it one bit, but Tom, or whoever he was, seemed intent on proving what a mature, stable, responsible individual he was.

Maybe she'd let him play his game out, and then she'd tell him to knock it off and be himself.

In front of the restaurant, a valet helped Sabrina out of the car and gave Tommy a claim ticket. The host, a short, balding man with a debonair moustache, greeted Tommy like an old friend.

"Ah, Mr. Cameron, so nice to see you again."

"Miles, good to see you too." Tommy and Miles shook hands.

Sabrina covered her surprise at such a familiar reception.

Miles gave Sabrina a big smile displaying lots of white teeth. "I have your table ready. Right this way."

Tommy pulled Sabrina's chair out for her and waited until she was settled before seating himself. Miles handed them each a menu and encouraged them to enjoy their dinner before he retreated.

Sabrina gazed around at the linen-covered tables, each with a spray of fresh flowers as a centerpiece. Several were occupied with well-heeled patrons who were obviously at home in such surroundings.

She brought her gaze back to Tommy who was perusing the menu. He looked comfortable in the restaurant's posh atmosphere.

"Do you come here often?" she asked as she opened her menu. He must, judging by the greeting Miles had given him.

"Occasionally. Usually with clients on expense accounts."

Not with other women? Sabrina wanted to ask. "Oh."

She fussed with the utensils of the elaborate place setting while a busboy filled their water goblets. A waiter appeared and listed the specials in rapid-fire succession. Sabrina, who'd already noticed the outrageous prices, barely paid attention.

Tommy nodded, requested iced tea for both of them, and asked for a few minutes before ordering their meals. The waiter bowed in deference.

Tommy took a sip of water and caught Sabrina looking at him. "What?" he asked.

"Who *are* you?" Sabrina didn't care if she couldn't string together more than three words at a time. She didn't care if Tommy knew he'd thrown her for a loop.

"I'm sorry. I thought we'd met." Tommy reached across the table and offered her his right hand. "Thomas Cameron. Pleased to make your acquaintance."

Sabrina scowled but automatically shook hands with him.

"Don't you think you're taking this 'Thomas' bit too far?"

Tommy glanced up from his menu. "What 'Thomas' bit?"

Sabrina slapped her menu down on the table, forgetting she'd planned to play along with Tommy's game. "I mean where's Tommy? You know, the guy whose dog digs up the neighbor's flowers? The one who throws impromptu parties with loud music?"

"He's been temporarily reassigned." Tommy couldn't quite contain the quirk of a grin at one corner of his mouth.

"Why?"

Tommy laid his menu aside and fixed Sabrina with his intense look. "Because the neighbors were complaining."

"Which neighbors?"

"Actually, it was only one. But there may have been some merit to her charges of uncouth and immature behavior."

"I never said you were uncouth!" Sabrina hissed.

"And I never said it was you," Tommy countered.

Sabrina sat back and crossed her arms and legs, her foot dancing up and down in agitation.

"So you decided to teach me—her—a lesson, is that it?"

Tommy smiled as the waiter approached. "Why Sabrina, haven't you heard? Every dog can be trained. It's just a matter of patience, consistency, and persistence."

Sabrina silently fumed as the waiter approached. "Are you ready to order?"

Tommy raised his eyebrows at Sabrina in silent question. "I'll have the prime rib with the shrimp."

Tommy made a murmur of what sounded like disapproval.

"What?" Sabrina asked.

"Nothing, nothing at all. Just a lot of calories in red meat. And you really should be careful of your cholesterol intake."

Cholesterol intake? This from a man who ate ribs and french fries, pizza and cream-filled snack cakes at every opportunity.

Sabrina smiled up at the waiter. "I'd like Bernaise sauce with that, if you have it, a loaded baked potato, and extra dressing on the salad. Oh, and could you bring some more butter for the rolls." She indicated the small pot of butter already on the table. "This won't be nearly enough."

"Very good, madam." The waiter appeared unfazed by her requests. He turned to Tommy. "And for you, sir?"

"I'll have the rainbow trout. Grilled. No butter. A plain salad and the rice pilaf."

Sabrina wanted to groan. She'd somehow managed to turn outgoing, fun-loving Tommy into this boring, stuffy fellow named Thomas. *I've created a monster,* she thought, wondering if it would be possible to change him back.

"So tell me about your work," Tommy said. He reached for a roll and put it on his bread plate, ignoring the butter.

"My work?" Sabrina echoed. Who *is* this guy?

"Yes. You've been teaching high school how long?"

"Six years."

"And do you enjoy it? How are your classes this semester?"

Sabrina took a sip of the freshly brewed iced tea. It really was very good. Too bad she couldn't say the same about the company. She decided to grin and bear it. In some way, she deserved this.

"Right now I'm teaching honors and advanced placement students. Introduction to Victorian Poetry. Nineteenth Century English Literature. Introduction to World Literature."

"Did you always want to teach?"

"I always wanted to be able to support myself. I wanted a job where I wouldn't have to relocate."

Tommy tilted his head to one side in interest. "Why?"

"My family moved often during my childhood, and I hated it. New schools, different houses, leaving friends and trying to make new ones." Sabrina tried to shake off the bad memories. "If I ever have children, they're going to grow up with some sense of security."

"And you think security comes from staying in one place?"

"I think it helps. But real security comes from knowing you're loved for who you are."

Thomas smiled, and Sabrina felt once again as if she'd passed one of his tests with flying colors. She wished she knew when he'd be handing down her grades.

Chapter Twenty

Tommy resisted the urge to run a finger around his collar in an effort to loosen it. Suits and ties, in his opinion, should be reserved for weddings and funerals.

He wondered which would be in his immediate future. If he shot himself in the foot, as he'd come close to doing a couple of times during his acquaintance with Sabrina, it would be his funeral. But if he played his cards right, he was pretty sure he could prove to Sabrina he was the right guy for her. Hadn't she just said real security comes from knowing you're loved for who you are?

He knew for a fact he loved Sabrina for who she was. She wasn't perfect, no matter how hard she tried to be, but then neither was he. He loved her matching outfits, her neat-as-a-pin house, and her collection of antiques and tea-pots. He loved her quirky mind and the way she sometimes made inaccurate assumptions about people. Joey Gianetti as a doctor! The memory made Tommy smile. Joey'd barely passed high school biology.

Although it took Sabrina a while to warm up, he could see now her initial coolness toward him was nothing more than a protective mechanism. She didn't want to be hurt. She didn't want anyone or anything to ruin the serene environment she'd achieved for herself.

"I won't do that," Tommy wanted to tell her. "I just want you to let me in. Permanently." He wasn't quite there, but he was definitely making progress.

Sabrina didn't want to be attached to people or places or things for fear it would all be yanked away from her. He vowed if she stuck with him, he'd never let that happen. He'd sell his house and move into hers. They'd grow old together in Oglethorpe, Illinois.

When their food arrived, Tommy noticed Sabrina didn't touch the Bernaise sauce she'd requested. She scraped most of the butter, sour cream, and other toppings off her baked potato, ate only half of her prime rib and most of the shrimp. The extra butter went untouched. In fact, she passed on the rolls when he offered them to her.

He smiled inwardly. That was another thing he loved about her—her efforts to defy him. Even when his suggestions went along with her natural inclinations.

Tommy talked her into sharing one of the Red Door's special hot fudge sundae concoctions, consisting of the restaurant's homemade ice cream and a warm nut-filled brownie.

Before dessert arrived, Sabrina excused herself to the ladies room.

Tommy watched as she made her way through the now crowded restaurant. She looked dynamite in that dress. He noticed more than one male head swivel in her direction as she negotiated between the tables.

Tommy clenched a fist, feeling his patience wear thin. He had to convince her they were right for each other. Soon. Very soon.

He hoped his transformation into *Thomas* would do the trick. If she'd wanted him to clean up his act as he'd suspected from the beginning, this ought to teach her a lesson. He was laying it on so thick, pretty soon she'd be begging to have good old Tommy boy back.

"Would you like to dance?" Tommy asked when they finished dinner. Live music could be heard from the lounge portion of the Red Door Inn. It wasn't a three-piece orchestra, but Tommy knew the band played lots of slow dance tunes.

"I'd love to." Sabrina gave him a hundred-watt smile and Tommy grew warm. The palms of his hands were damp. He wondered if he could maintain his proper Thomas façade once he had Sabrina in his arms on the dance floor. Could he resist the urge to hold her close and bury his nose in the fragrance of her hair?

He flexed his fingers as they made their way to the dance floor. Of course, he could control himself. He was *Thomas*. Mature, stable, responsible, stodgy Thomas Cameron who wouldn't think of doing anything improper on a first date. In fact, if all went as planned, he'd kiss her on the cheek at her door and wait the requisite three days before calling to ask her out again.

"They're playing our song," Tommy noted. They were on their third dance, and it was all Tommy could do to resist Sabrina's efforts to get closer to him.

He held her at bay with one hand on her waist and the

other firmly holding hers, exerting an equal measure of counter-pressure. Inwardly he groaned.

Unfortunately, it didn't seem to matter what kind of distance he maintained between them. Heat rose off her in waves, her subtle perfume tickling his nostrils and inflaming his imagination. He moved automatically to the music, but his mind was somewhere else. Pictures were taking shape in his head of a future with Sabrina. Roses climbed a trellis at the side of the porch. There were a couple of kids running around the front lawn. Skid was chasing them just before he ran off to dig up a rosebush. It all seemed real and achievable and right. Tommy shook himself out of the fantasy.

"Are you okay?"

Sabrina gazed up at him. Her tanzanite-tinted eyes were soft and smoky in the romantic lighting. Concern furrowed her brow.

"I'm fine," Tommy managed to say. What could he say? *It's just gas?* No wait. *It's a touch of heartburn.* Heartburn. It's more like a heart on fire. Is this what being in love did to a man? Tommy released Sabrina's hand for a moment and wiped the perspiration from his brow.

"Maybe you should take off your jacket. It's a bit warm in here," Sabrina suggested. "Are you sure you're okay?"

"I'm fine. Do you mind if we sit down for a minute?"

"No, not at all."

Sitting at one of the small tables surrounding the dance floor was a mistake, Tommy decided. He removed his jacket but felt little relief from the heat beneath his skin. Sabrina crossed her legs. The skirt of her dress slid up and clung mid-thigh. This time Tommy didn't ignore the urge to run a finger around the inside of his collar in an effort to loosen it and let some of the heat escape.

Sabrina's hair swept her shoulders as she moved slightly to the beat of the music. She seemed content to listen to the band and watch the other dancers. Tommy watched her.

Did she have any idea how sexy she was? Did she have any idea what she was doing to him?

Evidently not. She leaned toward him, the formfitting black dress clinging to every one of her curves. "Do you have anything in your repertoire besides slow dancing?"

Tommy managed to get his gaze back where it belonged, but his mind didn't follow as fast. "Huh?"

Sabrina motioned toward the dance floor and the band which had picked up the beat to an old disco tune. She tugged on his hand, and Tommy followed her lead. As if slow dancing hadn't frayed his self-control enough, dancing at a distance threatened to snap it completely.

He wasn't touching her, and he couldn't smell her perfume. But he could *see* her. And if anyone had told him demure, conservative Sabrina Talbott could dance the way she was dancing, he wouldn't have believed it. But he was seeing it with his own eyes. He tracked her arms and legs, the sway of her hips as she spun and twisted. He might have been standing still, so transfixed was he. Sabrina was having a good time. Tommy'd bet his life on it. Why then, was he so miserable?

Because he wanted to be alone with her. Away from the crowd of dancers and the smoky lounge. *Right now.*

"Are you okay?" Sabrina asked again as the song ended.

"I'm fine. Are you ready to go?"

The light in Sabrina's eyes went out, and Tommy wanted to kick himself at the look of disappointment on her face. But if he didn't get out of here now, he didn't think he could be held responsible for his actions.

"If you are," she answered.

They returned to the table for her purse, Tommy's jacket, and Skid's doggie bag which held a nice chunk of prime rib. Tommy left some cash for their drinks. They stood side by side not touching as they waited for the valet to fetch the car. The evening air was cool and Tommy felt some sense of sanity return. He'd make it up to Sabrina for ending the evening so abruptly. But right now, he had to get her home and get her safely inside her house. Before he ruined everything.

"Could you open the sunroof, please?" Sabrina asked once they were on their way.

"Gladly." Tommy pressed the button and the panel over their heads slid back. Cool autumn air rushed in, dispelling the scent of the rose Sabrina had left on her seat earlier.

She toyed with it now, feathering the petals with the tips of her fingers. Tommy did his best to keep his eyes on the road and his mind off Sabrina.

They were almost home before he noticed she'd been pulling the petals off the flower one by one and dropping them in her lap.

"What are you doing?"

Sabrina's head shot up as if he'd just discovered one of her deeply buried secrets.

"N—nothing. It's an old game. Sorry I made such a mess in your new car." Hastily she gathered the fallen petals. Raising her arm overhead, she released them through the sunroof where they disappeared into the night.

Tommy parked the car and opened Sabrina's door for her. Like the gentleman he was trying to be, he averted his eyes from her legs as she stepped out.

He walked her to her door, took her keys from her, and unlocked it. Leaning forward, he kissed her cheek, just as he had planned, marveling at the return of his self-control. "Good night, Sabrina."

"Good night, Tommy, uh, I mean, Thomas."

Was there a wistful note in her voice or had he imagined it? He put his hands in the pockets of his suit pants and quelled the urge to look back as he crossed the lawn. *Bree, darling, I think I've got you right where I want you.*

Sabrina closed the door behind her and slumped against it. Her clever plan to make herself irresistible to Tommy had failed. That Thomas. He'd ruined everything.

Victoria appeared and seated herself at the edge of the rug, eyeing her mistress for a moment before licking a paw. Sabrina looked down at the rose she'd destroyed. Only one petal remained. She tugged it off and finished the game.

He loves me not.

Chapter Twenty-one

Sunday morning found Sabrina in church, but her mind wasn't on the service or the sermon. Instead she mentally reviewed her date with *Thomas* the night before. Could Thomas possibly be as immune to her as he wanted her to believe? If so, he wouldn't have asked her out to begin with, would he? His choice of the Red Door Inn was a clear indication he'd wanted to impress her.

She wished she'd been impressed. She wished Thomas was the man of her dreams. He should be. My goodness, he said and did all the right things. Carried on intelligent conversation. Drove a nice, conservative sedan. Dressed well. Danced well. He was everything she'd expected Mr. Perfect to be. She'd never been so disappointed in her life. Presented with exactly what she'd been telling herself she wanted, she found out she didn't want it at all.

She turned the evening over and over in her mind. Why

do men take women to expensive restaurants? To woo
them, right?

Wrong. At least that hadn't been Thomas' intention.
He'd pecked her on the cheek and left her at her door.
Sabrina squirmed with frustration. What was wrong with
the man? She'd dressed to the nines for him. In fact, that
dress had "woo me" written all over it. Yet Thomas had
not made one move in that direction.

Sabrina made a decision as the minister offered the final
blessing. Thomas Cameron had to die.

Monday morning Elaine settled herself in the chair next
to Sabrina's desk with a full cup of coffee. They both had
a break between classes. "So? How was your date with
Tommy?"

"We went to dinner," Sabrina began.

"Where?"

"The Red Door Inn."

"The Red Door? Wow! Was it fabulous?"

"The food was very good."

"Uh-oh. What happened?"

"Nothing." Inexplicable sadness washed over Sabrina as
she admitted the truth to Elaine.

"Nothing, as in . . . ?"

"Nothing. Nada. Nothing happened. We ate. We danced.
He dropped me at my door and kissed me on the cheek!"

"On the cheek?" Elaine bit her lip and Sabrina sensed
she was trying not to laugh.

"What's so funny?"

Elaine held up a hand. "Nothing. Nothing, I swear."

"He wore a suit and tie, Elaine. Can you believe it? And
you know what he did?"

"What?" Elaine tried to school her features into a serious expression and almost made it.

"He showed up with a red rose. A single, perfect, red rose. Can you believe it?"

"Wow. That's so romantic. I'd swoon if a guy showed up at my door with a red rose."

Sabrina nodded. "Exactly."

"He really likes you, Sabrina. In fact, it sounds like he's in love with you."

"Huh!" Sabrina crossed her arms over her chest. "Well, he sure didn't act like it Saturday night. And you know what else? He got rid of his Jeep. He's got this four-door sedan. A sedan, Elaine. Leather interior, tinted windows, a roof."

"Hmmmm. Sounds awful." Elaine carefully sipped her coffee, trying to keep a straight face.

"And I looked hot, Elaine. You should have seen the dress I found. Black, clingy. You know what he said? He said I looked 'nice.' Nice! I looked way better than nice and he knew it."

"How did he look? In a suit, I mean?"

Sabrina groaned. "He looked incredible. Like Tommy, only different. But I think the suit affected his personality. Or maybe it was the haircut. He might have tied his tie too tight and cut off the flow of blood to his personality."

Elaine dug her teeth into her bottom lip.

"Maybe he just wanted to impress you."

Sabrina stared at her friend. "Impress me? Why would he need to impress me?"

"Oh, Sabrina, come on. Didn't you tell Tommy to his face that he was immature and irresponsible and that you wouldn't go out with a guy like him?"

"I didn't mean to—"

"And you didn't like his loud music or his parties. Or his friends."

"But that was before—"

"I know. That was before you got to know him. But maybe Tommy doesn't know that."

"Oh, no." Sabrina groaned. She'd have to prove to Tommy that she didn't want him to change. She'd have to make him see that she loved him just the way he was. And she knew the perfect way to do that.

"Elaine, remember my idea about having a party?"

Elaine nodded. "Inviting your friends to meet Tommy's friends? I still think it's a terrific idea."

"How about this weekend? Are you available to help me?"

Elaine lifted her mug in a toast. "Let's do it."

On Tuesday morning Sabrina stopped by Tommy's house on her way back from her power walk. There seemed no point in dressing to impress him if he wasn't going to notice. If the figure hugging black spandex crop top and matching leggings which stopped just below the knee didn't do it for him, that was just too bad.

She knocked on his door and shivered slightly as the cool autumn air chilled the light sheen of perspiration on her skin. She gazed around at Tommy's porch imagining how it would look with roses blooming on the trellis next summer. The white trim gleamed in the morning sun, a perfect complement to the pearl gray of the floor and steps.

The door opened and Tommy appeared. His sleepy gaze turned to one of full alert. "Skid, sit," he commanded when Skid was about to lunge through the screen to get to Sabrina.

The dog sat. Tommy flashed his palm in front of Skid's

face. "Stay," he commanded. Skid's tail wagged madly but otherwise he didn't move a muscle. His perceptive brown eyes flickered between his master and the visitor.

Sabrina's mouth went dry. Tommy was still in his pajamas—the white T-shirt and the drawstring bottoms. His hair was mussed and he hadn't yet shaved. He'd probably just gotten out of bed.

"Good morning," Tommy drawled.

It occurred to her that she hadn't said a word. She sure hoped she could think of one on such short notice.

"Hi," she responded brightly.

Several seconds went by. Sabrina became distracted by Tommy's bare forearms, which were crossed against the breadth of his chest, making the sleeves of his T-shirt strain at the shoulders. The waistline of his pajama bottoms rode low on his hips. Moisture returned to her mouth and she gulped.

"Want to come in? I'll make some coffee."

He opened the screen door in invitation.

Skid's head swiveled between Tommy and Sabrina, but he stayed where he was.

"Wow. Skid's being so good. He's like a different dog."

"Yeah. The new and improved version."

"Can I pet him?"

"Sure. Okay!" Tommy said to Skid. Released from the stay command, Skid sidled up to Sabrina. She bent over him, rubbed his chest, and ruffled the fur behind his ears.

"Oh, look at you. You're such a good boy, Skid. Such a good boy." She didn't notice the dog hair that clung like glue to the black spandex. Skid gazed up at her and whimpered in ecstasy.

Tommy shifted positions and cleared his throat.

Sabrina suddenly remembered why she was there. It

wasn't to see Skid. She straightened, and Skid stood looking up at her, tail wagging. Sabrina returned her attention
to Tommy.

"I'm having a party Saturday night."

"A party? You?"

"Yes me. You needn't act so surprised."

"No, I suppose not." Tommy glanced meaningfully at
the dog, probably thinking Skid wasn't the only one who'd
come a long way in a short time.

Sabrina didn't care. She had a mission.

"Will you come?"

Tommy's eyes lit up.

"Want me to bring anything?"

Bring Tommy, if you can find him in there somewhere.

"Just yourself," Sabrina told him.

Tommy nodded. "I'll be there."

Sabrina backed up a couple of steps. "See you Saturday,
then."

By 9:00 Saturday night, the party was starting to heat
up. The guests had overcome their initial awkwardness with
each other. Frank Long and Elaine were instrumental in
making introductions. Joey and Buddy were in a conversational foursome with Delia and Valerie.

Sabrina crossed her fingers as she made a pass through
the crowd. So far so good. She turned the music up a notch
and replaced an empty chip bowl with a full one. In the
dining room she put out another tray of cheese and crackers
and replenished the dip for the vegetables.

Tommy was late.

All of his friends were here. She wondered if anyone
else had noticed his absence.

Surely he wouldn't let her down. He'd accepted her invitation. Not once since she'd known him had he gone back on his word.

She returned to the kitchen just as the oven timer dinged. She removed the pan of buffalo wings and piled them on a tray.

"Great party, Sabrina." Delia Potter opened the refrigerator and removed a bottle of diet soda. "Where have you been hiding all these single bachelor friends of yours?" she teased as she poured.

"Does that mean you and Valerie approve of Buddy and Joey?"

"Are you kidding? We're in heaven. I can't remember when I've had a better time. Valerie's already fawning over Joey. He's a doll."

"She does know he's a plumber, doesn't she?" Sabrina inquired.

Delia rolled her eyes and giggled. "Yeah. I wouldn't be surprised if she invites him over to inspect her plumbing real soon."

Delia disappeared back into the crowd. Sabrina squeezed through behind her with the platter of wings. Which she almost dropped when she caught sight of Tommy. She set the wings down with a clatter and stared.

It was Tommy, wasn't it? Or was this Tom? Or another version of Thomas?

Whoever he was, she didn't like this new persona one bit.

She charged through the crowd until she was face to face with him.

Her gaze swept him from head to toe. "What kind of getup is this?"

"Pardon me?"

Sabrina gestured with her hand. "This! What is this?"

"My clothes?"

Tommy looked like a freak amongst the other guests. She'd emphasized casual dress in the invitations. She herself had donned stretch denim jeans that fit her like a second skin and a snug sweater that showed off her figure to its best advantage. She'd expected Tommy to notice her the second he saw her, but she'd seen him first. And whoever this guy was, noticing her was going to be the last item on his agenda this evening.

"What is this?" She tugged on his arm. He was wearing a gray cardigan sweater. A cardigan sweater! Over a buttoned-to-the-top long-sleeved white shirt. And black trousers that were a couple inches too short for him. She stared at his feet. What kind of shoes was he wearing? Saddle shoes? And were those argyle socks? *Argyle? Tommy?*

But that wasn't the worst of it.

"It's a sweater. It's a bit chilly out, in case you hadn't noticed."

Like chilly weather could ever induce Tommy Cameron to wear a gray cardigan. A hooded sweatshirt, she could see. A denim jacket, yes. But not this sweater. And not these socks. Or the trousers or the shirt or those awful shoes. He looked like a college professor. In fact, he reminded her of the stodgy old coot who taught science at the high school.

On top of that, his now short hair was parted in a straight line, slicked down and combed to one side in a style popular about forty years ago.

She stared into Tommy's eyes. "Since when do you wear glasses?" The heavy tortoiseshell frames and thick lenses gave Tommy a studious, serious look Sabrina didn't like at all.

"Would you believe I lost my contacts?"

"I think you've lost your mind." He'd certainly been instrumental in making her believe she'd lost hers. "Come with me." She grabbed his wrist and pulled him in the direction of the front door.

"You're kicking me out? But I just got here," Tommy protested.

Chapter Twenty-two

Sabrina gritted her teeth as she tugged him down the steps behind her. "I'm not kicking you out," she informed him as she stomped across the lawn toward his house. "I told you all you had to bring was yourself. And since you couldn't manage to do that on your own, I'm going to help you."

"You are?"

She opened the door to his house, never letting go of him. Skid rushed forward to greet them. She held up a hand to wave him off. "Not now, Skid."

She marched up the stairs, dragging Tommy behind her as if he were a wayward child. She turned the light on in his bedroom, dropped his wrist, and pointed to his attire. "You're going to change your clothes. Now."

"Sabrina—"

"Starting with these." She yanked the glasses off and

179

tossed them on the dresser. "And this." She ruffled his neatly combed and parted hair, messing it up. "Better."

She pointed to his clothes. "You do the rest."

She opened his closet and began rummaging through the contents. "I don't know who you are, if you're Tom or Thomas, but I don't like it. I don't like those clothes, and I don't like the way you act when you're wearing them."

As she spoke, she yanked the hangers along the rod searching for Tommy's clothes.

"I know I made some assumptions about you when I first met you. And I'll admit, the assumptions I made were wrong. But this has gone far enough."

Abandoning the closet for the moment, she opened the top drawer of a chest of drawers. She pawed through a haphazard pile of boxers and briefs before slamming the drawer shut.

Out of the corner of her eye she saw Thomas standing where she'd left him, watching her. "Take that sweater off. And unbutton your shirt."

She waited until she saw him start to shrug out of the sweater before she opened the second drawer. White T-shirts and pajama bottoms. Nope.

She moved on to the third drawer. "Aha!" Her fingers slid over the cotton T-shirts. She drew out a soft gray one that said Property of Athletic Department. "Here you go." She tossed it over her shoulder in Tommy's direction. The fourth drawer held only miscellaneous odds and ends. Not what she was looking for.

She moved on to the dresser. Tommy'd managed to get the sweater off and had the shirt halfway unbuttoned. She pointed to the shirt before attacking the dresser drawers. "Off."

The first drawer she tried rewarded her. Still she sorted

through the choices looking for the most worn, most faded, softest pair of jeans she could find. She tossed them on the bed where they landed next to the gray T-shirt.

The white dress shirt landed on the floor. On her way back to the closet she pointed. "Now those ridiculous shoes."

On her hands and knees, she stuck her head back into his closet. "Tommy, when I told you to come as yourself, I meant you. Tommy. You're not Tom. And you're not that boring Thomas character. You're Tommy."

Sabrina could feel herself getting choked up, but it had nothing to do with the fumes rising from the variety of beat-up sneakers buried in the depths of Tommy's closet. "I don't want Tom. And I don't want Thomas." She sniffed as she grabbed a pair of sneakers and clutched them to her chest. "I want Tommy," she said to the shoes. "I'm in love with Tommy."

She was almost afraid to turn around and look, hoping against hope that Tommy had somehow magically reappeared.

He had. At least she hoped it was him. It was kind of hard to tell since he was now wearing the gray T-shirt with the black trousers and the argyle socks.

Sabrina got to her feet still clutching the sneakers. "Tommy?"

Tommy, or Tom, or Thomas, was watching her intently. He didn't have that lazy look in his eyes. He had that glittering, intense, hot look. She was pretty sure Tommy was the only one of them who had that particular expression. The look that melted her bones and made her mind turn to mush with all kinds of crazy fantasies. The look that usually made her mouth go dry.

Her mouth went dry. She took a couple of tentative steps toward him. "Tommy?"

She dropped the shoes when he hugged her. Then he tickled her, his fingers quickly finding the most sensitive places. She howled in relief and shrieked with pleasure. "Tommy!"

He stopped tickling her and looked down at her. "What?" His eyes locked with hers.

Sabrina knew it was now or never. "I love you, Tommy."

Tommy nodded. "About time you figured that out."

"Oh, Tommy." She framed his face with her hands. "Don't ever change. I love you just the way you are."

"You do, huh? Well, I sure never thought I'd fall in love with a Miss Smarty Pants like you."

As declarations of love went, it wasn't exactly what she'd expect from Mr. Perfect, but Sabrina couldn't stop the smile that formed on her lips even as Tommy kissed her.

"Finally," she breathed when he lifted his head.

"Finally, what?" he asked before he began to nuzzle her neck.

"I finally found the man of my dreams."

"Uh-huh," Tommy whispered. "Disappointed?"

"No, not at all. I don't think I'll ever be disappointed in you." She melted a little more each time he kissed her, even when he started talking between kisses.

"So tell me, how would you feel," he asked. Kiss. "About marrying a man who's irresponsible?" Kiss. "Immature?" Kiss. "Unstable?" Kiss. "Uncouth."

"I never said you were uncouth," Sabrina reminded him.

He stopped kissing her. She blinked her eyes open. He had that serious, intent look on his face.

"But still, how do you feel about marrying a guy like that?"

Sabrina smiled. "I think it will be great. That guy is perfect for me."

Tommy grinned down at her. "Good."

Sabrina wrapped her arms around him in acceptance.

"Then you won't mind if I get rid of that car I drove the other night?"

Sabrina shook her head. "I won't mind. I won't mind at all," she answered dreamily.

"That's good. Because it was just a rental. My Jeep's in the garage."